MIKE PHILLIPS was born in Guyana, and moved to London in 1955 at the age of thirteen. He has worked as a teacher, and set up a hostel for black youths in London's Notting Hill.

More recently, he has been a journalist and broadcaster; he is currently a Senior Lecturer in Media Studies and Journalism at the Polytechnic of Central London.

He is the author of two novels featuring the investigator Sam Dean: *Blood Rights* (1989), which BBC Television filmed as a four-part series, adapted by the author; and *The Late Candidate* (1990), winner of the Crime Writers Association's prestigious Silver Dagger Award.

Mike Phillips lives in London, where he is currently writing his third Sam Dean novel, *Point of Darkness*, and a screenplay of *The Late Candidate*.

BOYZ N THE HOOD

JOHN SINGLETON, who makes his major motion picture writing and directing debut with *Boyz N The Hood*, grew up in South Central Los Angeles, the community that served as the inspiration for his script and provided the locations for the film's production.

'When I was growing up, my parents didn't have a lot of money,' Singleton says. 'My parents never married, and I used to see my father on the weekends and stay with my mom during the week. I used to steal little stuff, like candy, toys, and Players magazines, but I never got into anything too rough.'

Singleton, now 23, knew that he wanted to get into film when he saw *Star Wars* in 1977. In his high school years, he began to strengthen his writing skills.

'When I was in high school, somebody told me that the film business was controlled by literary properties, i.e., screenplays. After I heard that, I knew that I had to learn how to write, so I did.'

Singleton entered the University of Southern California's Filmic Writing Program in 1986. Before graduating in 1990, he won the prestigious Robert Riskin Writing Award and an unprecedented two consecutive Jack Nicholson Writing Awards. This led to his signing with the prestigious Creative Artists Agency while he was still a student (an unusual occurrence in the industry).

'*Boyz N The Hood* is about the strength from within,' Singleton says. 'It shows us as we really are. I wrote the character of Dough Boy with Ice Cube in mind to play him. Same with Larry Fishburne – I knew that I wanted him to play Furious. Everyone involved with this picture is here because their hearts are one with this story.'

BOYZ N THE HOOD

A NOVELIZATION BY
MIKE PHILLIPS
BASED ON THE MOTION PICTURE WRITTEN
AND DIRECTED BY
JOHN SINGLETON

A PAN ORIGINAL
PUBLISHED BY PAN BOOKS
LONDON, SYDNEY AND AUCKLAND

A Pan original
First published 1991 by Pan Books Ltd,
Cavaye Place, London sw10 9pg

1 3 5 7 9 8 6 4 2

Novelization © Mike Phillips 1991
Screenplay © Columbia Pictures Industries Inc 1991

ISBN 0 330 32539 6

Phototypeset by Intype, London
Printed in England by Clays Ltd, St Ives plc

PROLOGUE

The room belongs to a young boy. On the floor there are piles of comics, a few toys, and a football in the corner. On the walls there are posters of Black superheroes like Luke Cage – Powerman, the Black Panther, the Falcon, Storm, and Sir Nose with his Bop Gun. In between are posters of Parliament, Fun-kadelic, and George Clinton. Tre is lying on the bed sleeping the dead sleep of an exhausted ten-year-old. This has been a big day for him. Today he has come to live with his father, and he has spent most of it raking leaves off the front lawn. Drifting through the open window come the night sounds of the neighbourhood, the *whop-whop* of helicopter blades, the whining scream of police sirens, and the distant firing of automatic weapons. Tre is accustomed to these sounds because they are a normal part of night-time in South Central L.A. Besides he's too tired to stay awake. The TV is still switched on and the screen is crawling with an electrical snowfall while the noise of static fills the room. But none of this disturbs the boy.

1

Tre doesn't even stir when his father Furious comes into the room, goes over to the TV, and turns it off. Furious is a big man, over six feet with broad shoulders. He's in good shape, and he carries himself in a calm, relaxed manner. He watches Tre's profile for a moment, still feeling the delight he'd experienced when the boy's mother had told him. Now, at last, Tre was safe and sound under his roof.

He wakes the boy quietly, and tells him that it's time to go to bed. Then he leaves the room to fetch an extra blanket. Tre gets up slowly, undresses, climbs back into bed, and by the time Furious returns to spread the blanket over him he is fast asleep.

Furious goes to the open window and closes it. Then he makes his round of the house, checking the locks and shutting all the windows. In the kitchen he looks at the pile of dirty dishes in the sink and turns his back on them. He is just about to cross to the living-room windows when he hears a faint sound, and he goes back to the door of Tre's room. Tre is still asleep, his face pressed against the pillow. He might have turned over in bed, Furious thinks, or made some small sound, and he watches the boy, smiling a little at himself and at the way Tre's presence in the house has sharpened his protective instincts, even made him jumpy. He is hardly conscious of the proud smile on his face but as he stands there he is experiencing a new feeling. This caring is

2

love, he thinks. He has wanted this for a long time and now he is determined to do the best job he can of bringing up Tre to be a man. Lost in his thoughts he stands there for a long while watching Tre, until his eyes begin to droop shut. Then he shakes himself, walks over to the door of his bedroom, goes in and lies down. In a couple of minutes he's asleep.

The neighbourhood sounds grow fainter and fainter. Occasionally a car creeps past the house, its engine almost inaudible. By two o'clock in the morning the street is deserted, wrapped in silence.

It is about this time a man lopes quietly along the street. It is too dark to see his face but he's thin, dressed in a dark sweater, cheap corduroy pants, and Converse sneakers. As he goes, he turns his head from side to side, scanning the houses carefully. He spots the window that Furious has forgotten to close, but he walks past the house slowly, before he turns and moves back to it. He looks around one last time, then he's through in a second. Inside the window he is too nervous to wait, and starts to cross the living-room floor immediately. Stupid. Before he goes more than a few paces he stumbles into the coffee-table, and doubles up in pain.

Furious's eyes snap open immediately. Somewhere in his brain he registers the fact that he's still sleeping with a part of his attention focused on picking up unusual sounds, breaks in the pattern of the night, the way he did in Nam. He rolls out of bed onto his knees and feels under the bed. He opens the shoe box that he keeps there and takes out a .357 Magnum. He loads it hurriedly, his hands shaking with nerves as he shoves the bullets in.

Furious can't see it, but the intruder's reflection looms in the mirror above him. The intruder doesn't see Furious in the darkness, but he's somehow aware that something in the house has changed. Suddenly both of them hear a door closing. Tre has woken up and set out to make a bathroom run. He is a stranger in the house, and he doesn't notice the vibes, or the small signals which might have told him something was going down, so he has calmly walked into the bathroom and closed the door.

The intruder braces himself to make a move, and Furious springs silently into the hallway, aims his gun, and clicks off the safety. The intruder reacts immediately and dashes for the freedom of the front door. Furious jumps round the corner and looses off a couple, the Magnum banging off like a cannon. BOOM BOOM.

In the bathroom Tre jumps at the noise. As he does so he accidentally dribbles pee down his legs, and it takes a little while before he can settle himself and dash for the door.

Meanwhile Furious is cautiously approaching the

door. He has blown two large holes in it, and missed the intruder, who by now has gone. Home free.

The shots have awakened the neighbourhood and Furious can hear the dogs barking up and down the street. Controlling his reaction, he walks calmly out to the front yard and over to where he can see a sneaker which the intruder has lost in his hurry. He picks it up, and Tre comes out of the house to stand beside him. Automatically Furious reaches back to pat the boy's shoulder in a reassuring and protective gesture.

An hour later they are still there, sitting on the front steps waiting for the cops to arrive. Tre is cool. As always he has so much faith in his father's strength and power that after the first shock he's hardly been scared at all. Furious knows better, and the sneaker in his hands keeps on reminding him that only a short while ago he had nearly killed a brother. He holds the sneaker up and they look at it thoughtfully.

'Somebody must have been praying for that fool,' Furious says, 'cause I aimed right for his head.'

'You shoulda blew it off,' Tre says.

Furious looks at his son in surprise. This is how it starts, he thinks.

'Don't say that,' he says. 'I'm glad I didn't get em. I woulda just been contributing to killing another brother.'

Suddenly he's aware that they've been waiting a

very long time and that Tre should have been back in bed.

'Where the hell are these fools? We've been waiting for almost an hour.'

In the same moment an LAPD squad car comes racing up the street, its red and blue lights flashing. It parks by the kerb and two cops get out. But the first thing Tre notices is the sign on the squad car door, 'To Serve and Protect'. The next thing Tre sees is that like the squad car the police team is black and white.

'Officers Graham and Coffey,' the white one says. 'We got a call about a burglary here.'

'That was an hour ago,' Furious says.

Coffey is still eating a doughnut, and when Furious answers his huge fist grips tight round it. His eyes flash with anger.

'We didn't ask you that,' he says.

'Well I told you,' Furious replies. 'Besides, I don't like having my son sitting out here in the cold.'

'What happened, sir?' Graham asks. His manner is a little more polite than Coffey's and he looks embarrassed by his partner's asshole behaviour.

'Somebody broke into my house,' Furious tells him. 'I shot at him with my piece and he ran.'

'You didn't get em?' Coffey sneers.

Furious eyeballs him coolly.

'He'd be laid out right here in front of you if I did.'

'Anything stolen?' Graham asks.

Furious shakes his head, still looking Coffey in the eye.

'Good,' the Black cop says in the same harsh tone. 'No need to file a report.'

The police radio breaks into chattering sound, and Graham turns, walks round to the driver's seat and reaches in to answer its call. Coffey stays, still confronting Furious.

'You should have got him,' Coffey says suddenly. 'That would have been one less nigga we had to worry about here.'

Furious doesn't reply. He is struggling half-way between pity and contempt for the man, and Coffey knows it. The cop's eyes suddenly light on Tre and he gives him a friendly grin.

'How ya doing little man?'

Furious feels a wave of disgust and anger at the thought of this man touching Tre, and he gestures his son away and stares coldly into Coffey's eyes. Then he shakes his head, turns, and begins walking up the stairs.

'Something wrong?'

Furious turns at the sound of Coffey's voice and looks him in the eye once again. The two men lock glances, until Furious breaks the silence.

'Yes,' he says, not bothering to hide his contempt. 'Yes, there is. Too bad you don't know it.'

CHAPTER ONE

When Tre thought about his move to the neighbour-hood seven years ago, he usually remembered the happenings of the day before, because in his mind that was how it had all started. When he woke up that day in his mother's apartment in Inglewood everything was normal. Outside he could hear the usual morning sounds, birds chirping, dogs barking, car horns. Around him were the familiar objects, on the wall the posters he'd put up with his mother, Spiderman, the X-men, the Incredible Hulk. He'd only just opened his eyes when his mother came in. She was moving fast as usual, and as usual she was cheerful and happy, all the way up, even at that early hour.

'Good morning to you!' Reva was singing as she moves around the room. 'Good morning to you! Good morning, good morning, good morning to you! Time to get up!'

Quickly she pulls open the blinds sending the rays of sunlight flooding through the room, and directly into his face.

'I'm already up,' Tre said, keeping his eyes shut tight.

'Then open your eyes.'

Tre does so.

'Good! That's better,' Reva said straightening up ready to leave. 'I have a class till seven tonight so be in by five. I'll call to make sure. Don't forget to brush your teeth, wash your face, and comb your hair. There's something to eat on the stove for you. Bye.'

'Bye,' Tre said, sitting now on the edge of the bed, but still drowsy and drooping.

Reva goes out and he closes his eyes and crawls back under the covers. But Reva knows him too well to let him get away with that. In a moment the door opens again, and she comes in, throws the covers back, and jerks him out of bed.

'Get up, little boy!' she cries.

About an hour later Tre is waiting on a corner on Lawrence Street. He looks round impatiently but in the next minute he's joined by three other children. They're all the same age, ten years old, and in the same class at school. Trina and Keisha are about the same height, but the difference in their personalities is already outstanding. Trina is a little girl who seems self-assured and a little aloof, as if she had her own apartment. Keisha is shy and timid. Bobby is different again. He looks and acts like a budding criminal,

10

as if he's been studying and carefully memorizing the teenage gangsters he sees on the street.

The kids begin walking together towards school. As they walk a pack of stray dogs run past. In their constant search for food, they knock over and scrabble through the trash cans in their way.

'What's up, Tre?' Bobby asks. 'You do your homework?'

'What homework?' Tre replies. 'Not for real, yeah. I did it.'

'Can I copy it?' Bobby asks, his eyes pleading.

'Hell no,' Tre says ruthlessly. 'Too bad, you should have done it yourself.'

Bobby glares at him, but Trina, feeling the tension, tactfully changes the subject.

'Did y'all hear them shooting last night?'

'Yeah I heard it,' Tre says. 'I got under my bed.'

Bobby looks at him with contempt.

'You a scarycat.'

'My momma says a bullet don't have no name on it,' Trina tells him in a mildly reproving tone.

'I ain't afraid to get shot,' Bobby says, boasting. 'Both my brothers have been shot and they still alive.'

'They lucky,' Tre says, coming back at him.

The kids walk along for a moment in silence. Then Bobby breaks the ice.

'Y'all wanta see something?'

'What?' Tre asks him.

They all stop and stare at Bobby. He stares back, practising the blank, cold, gangster expression.

'I ain't saying what,' he says. 'Do you want to see it or not?'

The kids all nod yes. Without a word Bobby turns and leads them round the nearest corner to the alley-way running down the middle of the block. Lining the alleyway is a long row of garages. In each port there is trash, the waste products of the people's daily lives, piled high up towards the ceilings. One pile is sectioned off with yellow tape which reads DO NOT CROSS. Behind it are more stray dogs sniffing and licking at the ground. Tre shouts at them and waves his arms and they scatter, one or two of them growl-ing and baring their teeth. Meanwhile Bobby pulls the tape away and leads them into the garbage heap.

'What you going to show us?' Tre asks him. 'A bunch of fishheads?'

Bobby gives him a dangerous look.

'I know who was doing the shooting last night.'

'Yahhh! Yahhh!' Tre chants. 'Get outta here!'

Bobby pulls up the tape. Tre frowns and kicks over some rubbish to reveal several bloody spots, garbage covered with blood. There are also several pieces of grey matter scattered about. The girls gasp in horror. Keisha, more affected than Trina, shrinks

12

away from the sight. Tre looks on with indifference. This is a familiar sight.

'Is that blood?' Trina asks. 'What happened?'

'What do you think!' Bobby says sarcastically. 'Somebody got smoked! Look at the holes in the wall! You stupid!'

'Least I can tell my times tables!'

This is a taunt to which Bobby has no reply and Trina turns coolly to Tre.

'Look, why is the blood turning yellow?'

'That's what happens when it separates from the plasma,' Tre tells her.

'What's plasma?' Bobby asks, trying to get back into the conversation, but Trina and Tre both ignore him.

'Can we go now,' Keisha says.

She's moved to the edge of the group, and she's begun to cry. But Trina hasn't finished yet.

'What's all that grey stuff?'

'That's his brains,' Tre says.

Keisha begins to cry even louder now. She runs off down the alley. Tre runs after her. But he doesn't catch up with her until she's way down the alley and then she slows up and cringes near a garage door. By now she's weeping loudly, crying her heart out. Tre goes over and holds her.

'Don't cry Keisha,' he says as comfortingly as he can, kicking himself for not remembering.

'I . . . I . . . They shot my brother,' Keisha sobs helplessly.

Trina and Bobby join them.

'What's wrong with her?' Bobby says.

'Her brother got smoked last year,' Tre tells him, with a look on his face that dares the other boy to say something stupid.

But this piece of news silences even Bobby, and the three kids stand there for a moment, listening to Keisha cry, and waiting for her to get herself together so they can go on in to school.

A couple of hours later they're all in Mrs Olaf's fifth-grade classroom. Like every fifth-grade classroom the walls are covered with the children's paintings and illustrations. Life in South Central L.A. But these paintings look like Beirut. Mostly they are funeral scenes, helicopters, gang graffiti, stick-men gambling, fighting, shooting up the place, fancy cars owned by dope dealers, Mercs, Cadillacs, smoked-glass limousines. One drawing says in big dramatic letters: INCREASE THE PEACE.

Mrs Olaf, a skinny, fair-haired white lady in her mid-forties, is giving a history lesson, pointer in hand. She has a discontented expression and a patronizing manner towards her students. All of them are black or hispanic, and with the sharpness of children who understand prejudice almost by reflex they

14

realize that her condescension towards them is partly because she is dissatisfied with her own position in the world. Most of the children are quiet or paying attention, but Tre, lost in a world of his own, is drawing a picture of a Black superhero named Blackman, muscles bulging and with a huge B outlined on his chest.

'And so that's why,' Mrs Olaf says, 'we celebrate Thanksgiving, to commemorate the unity between the Indians – oops – I mean the native Americans and the early English settlers who were called . . . ? Class?'

The class knows its role and the kids chorus in unison.

'The Pilgrims!'

'Yes, the Pilgrims!'

Tre doesn't look up from his drawing but he throws his comment into the pause after the teacher has spoken.

'The Penguins!'

For a moment Mrs Olaf is shocked.

'Who said that?'

The class laughs and points to Tre.

'Mr Styles.'

Tre looks up.

'That's me.'

'Why is it you always have something funny to say?'

Oddly enough Mrs Olaf would really like an answer to this question. She always has the uneasy and frustrating feeling that Tre is more intelligent than she knows, and she would like to get through to him, but his style is to push her away, keep her out.

'Cause I'm a comedian!' he answers.

The class laughs and Tre's lips curve in a smile of secret satisfaction. Typical, Mrs Olaf thinks, and hopeless. In a few years he'll be running round the streets robbing and shooting at people. She controls her temper with difficulty.

'Would you like to teach the class,' she says sarcastically.

The class goes 'Oooh!' at this challenge.

'Yeah, I can do that,' Tre says casually.

Mrs Olaf is taken aback. She'd meant to crush Tre with her reply, but now the only way of saving face is to go through with it.

'Very well then, come up here and instruct us.'

Tre coolly walks up to the map. Bobby sits near by. It is evident that he is jealous. Tre has caught the attention of the entire class. Milking the situation Tre indicates the pointer.

'Can I have that?'

He begins to speak but Mrs Olaf stops him.

'What will be the basis of your lecture?'

'What?' Tre says, taken aback.

Mrs Olaf enunciates carefully.

'What are you going to talk about?

'I'm gonna tell you,' Tre says, 'if you let me talk! Shoot!'

The class laughs.

'OK. All right,' Tre says, 'does anybody know what the name of this place is?'

The pointer is on the continent of Africa.

'That's Africa, I know that,' Trina says.

'That's right, that's Africa,' Tre says. 'But did you know that Africa is the place where they found the body of the first man?'

'Yeah,' Bobby says. 'I know dat. I heard it in a song once.'

Tre goes on.

'My daddy says that makes it the place where all people originated from, that means everybody is really from Africa.'

He gestures with the pointer.

'Everybody, all of y'all, everybody.'

'I ain't from Africa, I'm from Crenshaw Mafia!' Bobby says loudly.

He throws up a gang sign.

'Like it or not you from Africa,' Tre tells him steadily.

'I ain't from no Africa,' Bobby says. 'You from Africa! You African booty scratcher!'

The class laughs. Tre is humiliated. His mother

has taught him that scratching your behind in public is disgusting, and he never does it. He saves face by throwing some of them a nasty look. Immediately they go silent.

'Punk, I'll kick your ass,' Tre says.

Mrs Olaf can see the situation is about to get out of hand and breaks in.

'Now, now boys, breathe in and out and count to ten, remember?'

The two boys ignore her. The tension between them is flaring. The class holds its breath.

Bobby gets up and faces Tre up close.

'I'll get my brother to shoot you in the face!'

'Get your punk-ass brother, bitch, I'll get *my* daddy. Least I got one, muthafucka.'

'I ain't nobody's bitch,' Bobby returns. He's in a blind fury. 'You a bitch, Bitch! You a bitch, your daddy's a bitch, and your momma's a bitch! Bitch!'

Suddenly, Tre strikes Bobby on the head with the pointer. They go head-up into a brawl. Mrs Olaf attempts to pull them apart, while the rest of the class is up in arms instigating on one side or another.

'Now, now, now! Calm down!' Mrs Olaf screams.

'Get your hands offa me, bitch!' Tre screams back at her.

Mrs Olaf's face turns tomato red. There is fear in her eyes and she steps back quickly. The class falls silent, not certain what they've just seen, but they know that Tre is in trouble.

Reva isn't surprised to get a call from Mrs Olaf, although she'd been hoping that Tre's recent behaviour was a phase and that now he would keep out of fights and quarrels. But the patronizing tone of the teacher's voice is getting her angrier and angrier, and she's struggling to keep her temper.

'Well, it's not as though he is a lost case, he's a highly intelligent little boy,' Mrs Olaf says.

'And you're a very perceptive woman,' Reva replies drily.

'Thank you,' Mrs Olaf says, missing the sarcasm. 'As I was saying, he's highly intelligent, and his vocabulary is enormous, it's just . . . '

Her voice trails off.

'Yes, go on,' Reva says, wondering where this is going.

'It's just he has a very bad temper. It makes it hard for him to interact with the other children. Maybe I can recommend therapy or a child psychologist or something.'

'No thank you,' Reva says, 'we can manage just as well.'

'Is there some problem in the home?' Mrs Olaf grinds on. 'Are you employed?'

19

By now Reva's blood is boiling at the insolence of the woman. But she holds it in.

'It really is none of your business,' she says, 'but since you asked, I am employed and I am studying to receive my master's degree.'

The surprise in Mrs Olaf's voice comes over clearly.

'So you *are* educated.'

Reva's had enough.

'Listen, are we gonna talk about me or my son?'

Mrs Olaf has heard the warning signals and she checks herself.

'I'm sorry. Well I'll be happy to see Tre back in class on Tuesday. His suspension is only for three days you know.'

Reva has been saving up for this part and she says it carefully, setting the teacher up.

'No, I don't think you'll be seeing Tre at all.'

'Why not, may I ask?' Mrs Olaf says, puzzled.

'Because Tre is going to live with his father.'

'His father.'

The same insultingly obvious surprise again.

'Yes. His father,' Reva says, giving her words a vicious edge. 'Or did you think we made babies on our own?'

Without giving Mrs Olaf a chance to answer, she slams the phone down. She is in such a rage that she doesn't notice at first that Tre has walked in, heard the last part of the conversation and is standing there smiling.

'Did you tell her where to go, Momma?'

Reva whirls on him.

'What was our agreement,' she says. 'What did we put down in writing?'

She goes over to the mantel, picks up a piece of paper, and shows it to him. Then she reads it aloud.

'I, Tre Styles, being of sound mind and body, agree not to get into any disputes whether physical or verbal for the rest of the school year. If I do not conform with this agreement I will go to live with my father, Mr Furious Styles. Signed Tre Styles.'

She looks closer.

'You have to work on your handwriting.'

Tre sighs and lowers his head. This time, he knows, she is serious, and in his bones he realizes that his life is about to undergo a great and serious change.

CHAPTER TWO

The next day Reva is driving Tre down Crenshaw Boulevard towards his father's house. Tre looks in curiosity at the action on the 'strip', but Reva is preoccupied, dead serious, and on the edge of tears.

'I just don't want to see you end up dead or in jail or drunk in front of some liquor store,' she says. 'Can you understand that?'

Tre nods slowly. He's seen those things too often not to understand.

'I love you,' Reva says. 'You are my only son.'

The tears begin rolling down Tre's cheeks. They come slowly at first but then heavily. Reva pulls the car over and holds him in her mothering arms.

A short while after they're driving into High Point Avenue. Tre still looks serious but he's got himself under control now. The street is quiet. Several neighbours are out in front watering the grass, others are out on their porches watching the world go by. One of the sights in the street is a bunch of eight boys playing street football. Among them is Ricky, a kid Tre knows, but Ricky's too busy right now to notice.

A little further on another bunch of kids are riding skateboards. One of them is Dough Boy, a strong, porky-looking, honey-toned kid, and the leader of the pack. When Tre sees him he waves, and Dough Boy waves back, then starts following the car.

'Who is that?' Reva asks, her attention caught.

'My friend,' Tre answers, his eyes still on Dough and his gang. 'We call him Dough Boy.'

He's feeling better already, Reva thinks as she parks outside Furious Styles's house, and for the moment she doesn't know whether to be glad or sorry about this.

As the car stops Furious looks up from raking the leaves in the yard and comes to the kerb. He's tall and good looking, about thirty, with serious brown eyes, like a larger version of Tre's. He sticks his head in through the car window.

'Howya doing?' he greets Reva.

'Doing fine. Yourself?'

'I'm living,' he says lightly, but there's an undertone of seriousness to it. 'That's enough for me.'

Reva nods. She still has a soft spot for Furious, but both of them know that it makes sense to be as cool as possible about the situation.

'Well. Here he is.'

Tre is still eyeing the gang peering around his father's body.

'You can't say hello?' Furious asks.

Tre focuses for the first time on his father's face and smiles.

'Hello Daddy.'

Furious relents.

'Go on and talk to your friends.'

Tre hops out the car dragging his bags behind him and goes over to Dough Boy, while Furious takes his place in the passenger seat.

'Well, there's your son,' Reva says. 'You wanted em. You got em.'

'Why are you making this so easy?' Furious asks. In his mind are all the times she'd told him that she could never be separated from her son.

Reva sighs thoughtfully.

'Hey, it's like you told me. I can't teach him how to be a man. That's your job.'

Reva forces a smile, looking out of the window at Tre talking to Dough Boy and the other kids. She notices the shortest one who has a small jeri curl in his hair and pretty regular features. She notices, also, that Tre is watching the car with a trace of sadness still in his face.

If the other boys notice it too they aren't saying.

'Yeah, I remember you,' Chris, the boy with the

25

jeri curl tells Tre. 'You collect all those comic books. You living here now?'

Tre nods a yes, watching his parents talking in the background.

'You still collect comic books?' Dough Boy says, amazed. He turns the look of astonishment on his friends. 'Boy, this fool got more comic books than a muthafucka.'

On the other side of the car Tre catches sight of Ricky throwing a pass, and so his attention is distracted at the very moment that Furious gets out of the car and Reva beckons to him.

'Tre! Come here,' she calls when she realizes his gaze is fixed somewhere else. Tre switches back to her and starts towards the kerb calling back to Dough Boy.

'Watch my stuff.'

He goes to his mother's side of the car and just then Ricky runs backwards towards them and catches another pass. He looks round at Tre, grinning.

'What's up Tre?'

Tre waves eagerly.

'What's up Rick?'

Reva watches all this soberly.

'Well it looks as if you've got all your friends here,' she says.

Tre nods.

'When are you coming to pick me up?' he asks.

'Whenever you want me to,' Reva says. 'Just call.'

She means it, but Tre knows that now he's made the move, asking to go back would hurt both his parents in different ways and make life difficult for all of them. But he's still glad to hear her say it. Reva leans out and kisses him, her lips lingering on his cheek. Then she gives him a long, serious look.

'Listen,' she says, 'this is just a temporary thing. When I get outta school I'll get a better job and a place to stay, maybe a house, then you can come back and things will be better. OK?'

'OK Mommy,' Tre says.

Reva touches him for one last time and then pulls away from the kerb. Tre watches her go, feeling alone for the first time in his life. Then he turns slowly and walks back to the lawn where his father is talking to Dough Boy and Chris.

'A business proposition?' Dough Boy is saying doubtfully as Tre approaches.

'That's right,' Furious says. 'Five dollars for the whole lawn. With not one leaf on it.'

'Five dollars,' Chris says, laughing. 'That ain't shit. I can make more'n that doing nothing.'

'Doing what?'

'He works for his uncle,' Dough Boy cut in hurriedly, giving Chris a warning glance.

Furious notices but doesn't pursue it.

27

'That's too bad,' he says. 'I can get my son to do it.'

'Do what?' Tre asks.

'Rake these leaves off the lawn.'

Tre looks at his father as if he's crazy. But Furious frowns straight down at the boy, laying the force of his will on him.

'Boy,' he says clearly. 'Don't you look at me funny when I say do something.'

He gives him the rake.

'There's two trash bags right there on the ground.'

He picks up Tre's large suitcase with one muscular arm and starts into the house.

'Later.'

The kids watch him go, and Dough Boy is the first to speak.

'Damn,' he says. 'Your daddy mean. He worse than the boogey man himself. You gotta do all these leaves. Who he think you is? Kunta Kinte?'

Chris doesn't know who Kunta Kinte is, but he knows it's something to do with slavery, and looking at the rake in Tre's hand he figures Dough Boy must be right. Time to leave.

'Well, see ya later,' he says.

The two boys move off down the street.

'What you mean? The boogey man?' Chris says to Dough Boy as they go. 'There ain't no boogey man.'

28

'Shut up, fool,' Dough Boy snaps back. 'Yeah there is.'

Chris has the final word.

'If there is I betcha the Hulk could whip his ass.'

As they go further down the street their voices fade, until Tre can't hear what they're saying.

'Yeah, later,' he mumbles. Gripping the rake he wonders whether he'll have to do this every day, but for the moment there is no way that he's going to disobey his father, so he bends down and begins work.

It's night-time before Tre is finished. By then he's collected two huge bags full of leaves. When he gets back in to the house it's nearly time for dinner and Furious is about to serve it up. Tre looks at the kitchen and his heart sinks as he realizes that it will probably be his job to clean it up. It is a pig's dream. The floor is unswept and the sink is piled high with heaps of dirty dishes.

Furious doesn't seem to notice the mess and he brushes past Tre to take three TV dinners out of the oven. One is for Tre, the others are for himself.

'Go wash your hands,' he says.

In the bathroom Tre washes his hands. Then, out of curiosity, he pulls back the shower curtain to look at the bathtub. It turns out to be worse than the kitchen. A thick black ring of old body dirt and dead skin runs round it, and as he looks at it Tre shakes his head in shame.

When he gets back to the kitchen Furious has nearly finished his first TV dinner and is about to start on the next one. Tre sits down and bows his head in prayer as he always does, while Furious watches him, a curious smile crossing his face. He waits till Tre has finished his prayer before he speaks.

'Ordinarily I cook,' Furious says. 'But I didn't have time to clean up before your mother called. You know how to cook?'

Tre nods.

'What do you know to make?' Furious asks, smiling.

'Meatloaf,' Tre mumbles, his mouth full. 'À la Reva.'

'À la Reva, huh. She taught you how to make it?'

'Yup,' Tre says. 'Almost as good as she does it.'

Furious raises his eyebrows at his confidence.

'Hmm,' he says. 'That's good.'

A silence. Furious can't think what to say for the moment, and Tre is busy with his dinner.

'Want some more Kool Aid?' he asks eventually.

Tre nods his approval and Furious pours him a cup. He observes himself doing this with a feeling almost of surprise. If he'd been eating with a woman, he thought, he'd have been the one to be served, but now, because Tre was his child he was the one doing the serving, and the weird thing is that doing it gives him a warm feeling of pleasure.

Later on, Furious is doing his nightly exercises. He is lying on the weight-lifting bench in the centre of the living-room, and pressing about two hundred pounds, up and down, pushing the bar up from his chest the full stretch of his muscular arms. Watching his father's biceps bulge and swell, Tre picks up a small wrist weight and begins trying to emulate his father. Furious looks over, then between breaths begins speaking. His tone is serious but friendly.

'Listen,' Furious says. 'I gotta lay down the rules of the house. Same thing as the weekends, you remember?'

Tre nods.

'What are they?'

Tre answers right away. He knows the rules by heart.

'Be in the house by seven o'clock. Which is better'n Momma – she says five. Do my chores. Wash the dishes. I gotta wash those in there?'

He knows he has to, and Furious simply nods.

'Shit,' Tre mumbles.

'What did you say?' Furious gives him a sharp look.

'Nuthin.'

'Watch your language,' Furious says. 'What's the rest of it?'

'Clean the bathroom sink, floor, and tub. I gotta clean that tub?'

'Yeah.'

Furious puts the weight back on the rest and flexes his arms. Tre shakes his head ruefully.

'Clean my room, water the lawn.' He pauses, thinking about Dough Boy's Kunta Kinte remark. 'Can I ask you something?'

'Yeah what,' Furious says. He knows what's coming.

'What do you have to do around here?'

Furious raises himself up to look at Tre. The kid's testing me, he thinks, with a feeling of pride.

'I don't have to do nothin but pay the bills, bring home the food, and put clothes on your back.'

Tre thinks about it.

'Glad I don't have to pay no bills,' he says, and suddenly he and his father find themselves smiling at each other.

Furious reaches into his pocket and takes out a five-dollar bill. As Tre takes it he gives a wide grin of pleasure.

'Thanks,' he says.

Furious shares the smile, then his expression turns serious.

'It may seem like I'm being hard on you but I'm not. I'm just trying to teach you how to be responsible. Your little friends don't have nobody to show them that. You'll see how they end up. Ya know Tre, you're a prince. I'm King and you're the Prince.'

He reaches over and tries to lift Tre, then makes a show of finding him too heavy.

'Damn. You getting big. That's my boy.'

Furious sits up on the bench. The exercises are over.

'And the King says it's time for the Prince to go to bed.'

Tre nods and both of them get up and go down the hallway towards their bedrooms. Furious goes in, lies on his bed, picks up a book from the nightstand and begins reading. Tre walks into his own room, turns on the TV, and picks up a comic book. Through the open window he can hear the night sounds of South Central L.A., the distant sounds of people shouting obscenities, automatic gunfire, and the piercing noises of police vehicles and helicopters. But somehow the sounds don't scare him, here in his father's house. Slowly his eyes begin to close.

The next morning when Tre woke up he remembered the scene and the big gun blasting off as if it had been a dream. But when he went out to look at the door he knew it had happened for real. Furious was gone by now and Tre decided to go over and see what Dough Boy was doing. He crossed the road going past an ice-cream truck which had just stopped, and entered the gate of Mrs Baker's house with some reluctance.

He can hear the sound of Mrs Baker's voice booming out at Dough Boy.

'You ain't shit, you just like your Daddy! Ain't going to do shit, ain't going to be shit. All you do is eat, sleep, and shit around here! Y'all must think I'm a maid the way you act.'

Tre shrank back out of sight.

'Is that it?' Dough Boy's voice said. 'I got to go.'

'Hell naw, that ain't it! It ain't it till I say it's damn it! You trying to get smart with me? Knock your ass into next week! Is that it? And where you going? You little fat fuck? Your little ass ain't got no job.'

Just then Mrs Baker sees Tre through the screen door.

'Who's this little fucka sitting on my porch?' She shouts getting off the couch where she's been lying to get a better look at Tre as well as to see anything in the neighbourhood that needs seeing.

'Oh,' Mrs Baker says when she's had a good look at Tre. 'You Furious's little boy, huh? When your Daddy going to come play some cards? I know he don't think he too good to come around no more. Too busy shooting up people.' She pauses. 'He still got that same girlfriend?'

Suddenly, Ricky with his football in hand comes

from behind his mother, saving Tre from her mouth and her questions.

'Excuse me momma.'

Ricky never has any trouble with his mother, unlike Dough Boy. The truth is that they have two different fathers and while Mrs Baker treats Ricky with love and affection, she treats Dough Boy with anger and contempt.

As Ricky comes out Tre runs off the porch and into the yard to go for a pass. Ricky throws him one which he catches gracefully. Tre runs towards him as if to fake him out. Ricky catches him and they share a laugh.

'Why you always be playing football?' Tre asks him.

Ball in hand, Ricky stops as if he almost has to think out his answer, but it comes quickly.

'Cause that's what I'm going to be.'

At this moment Dough Boy comes from behind his mother and crosses the porch without even bothering to acknowledge her presence. He joins Tre and Ricky on the sidewalk.

'Yo, I heard Furious shot at somebody last night. He get em?'

'No,' Tre says absently. His attention has strayed across the street to a mother and daughter, about his own age, who are pulling groceries out the back of their car. The girl has long hair bound in one large pigtail and wears what looks like the uniform of a private school. Tre doesn't know it yet but she is the neighbourhood sweetheart.

'Who's that?' he asks.

'That's my lady homeboy,' Dough Boy says.

'Her name's Brandi.'

'She ain't your woman, that's my woman,' Ricky says.

'How can she be your woman when she my lady?'

'She's my wife,' Ricky returns.

Tre takes no notice of the argument because he has caught Brandi's eye from across the street and she returns his interested glance with a smile.

Dough Boy and Ricky have started wrestling in the mean time.

'She may be your wife,' says Dough Boy, 'but I stick my dingaling in her every night so that make her mine.'

Tre is still watching Brandi but now her mother pulls her away into the house.

'Get your fast ass in here,' she says loudly, 'and quit looking at them nappy-headed boys!'

The door shuts behind them, and Tre turns round to see Dough Boy and Ricky wrestling in the grass. They stop when they see him looking.

'You can't have her cause we sharing already,' Dough Boy says.

*

A little while later they are walking into Nickerson Gardens Housing Project. This is one of the most notorious housing projects in South Central L.A., with a transient population of people who live in a mix of daily drug peddling and nightly murders.

The three boys walk freely through a maze of older boys, who are cursing, shouting, and drinking forty-ounce bottles of malt liquor. Tre looks at everything out of the corner of his eye. Dough Boy moves easily as if he's at home in this atmosphere. Ricky holds his ball close to his chest. Dough Boy looks at him and shakes his head.

'Rick,' he says. 'Why'd you haveta bring that ball? I ain't saying nothing if it get took.'

In a couple of minutes they are at the door of Chris's house. Dough Boy knocks confidently and Chris opens the door and invites them in.

It is a one-bedroom apartment. There are cracks as old as two grandfathers ingrained in the ceiling. Tre can see cockroaches crawling in and out of the crevices. On the couch below them Donetta, Chris's mother, is lying back watching the Saturday morning cartoons on an old large twenty-five-inch black and white set. She has permanently pressed hair and a face that makes her look ten years older than she is. She is flicking her cigarette ash into an ashtray from which two or three cockroaches emerge as the boys enter. She rouses herself enough to ask who they are and Chris tells her. These are his friends.

'Why don't y'all play outside,' Donetta says. 'I just cleaned up.'

The four boys leave and begin walking down the street.

'Somebody got smoked today,' Chris says conversationally.

'Where?' Dough Boy asks.

Chris points.

'Around that end. Wanta see? The people still ain't come to pick it up. He still on the ground dead to the world.'

They begin walking in that direction, while Dough Boy tells Chris about Tre's Daddy blasting on somebody the night before. Chris looks at Tre as if he's a new discovery.

'Really? What kinda gun your Daddy got?'

Tre says he thinks it's a .357 Magnum and Chris tells him that he has a .22, deuce-deuce, which his brother gave him before he went into the County jail.

'Got it under my bed. Wanna see it? It's loaded too.'

On the piece of waste ground that Chris has pointed out is a dead seventeen-year-old boy, his body riddled with bullets. Near by people are walking back and forth about their business taking no more notice than if this was the body of a dead dog.

'Look like Freddy Kruger got em,' Dough Boy says.

'This ain't the movies,' Ricky tells him.

'He stinks,' Tre says.

'That's how they smell after a while.' Chris is showing off his knowledge. 'I wonder why it take them so long to pick them up?'

Suddenly there's a voice behind them.

'Hey, throw that ball.'

They turn, startled, to see an older boy, about seventeen years old. He is bare-chested and wearing old corduroys, pulled down to reveal the top of his underpants.

'You throw that ball you ain't going to see it again,' Chris whispers to Ricky.

'Hey, you know this a dead body?' Tre shouts, hoping to distract the older boy, who, in reply, simply gives him a narrow-eyed gangster stare.

'Yeah muthafuckas, I know dat, shit! He ain't bothering you so don't fuck with him! Yo, throw the ball little man, I ain't going to take it. Little Chris, tell this fool I ain't going to take his ball, I gotta enough money to buy me a hundred balls. Shit!'

He flashes a couple of dollars, but the four boys realize that they're in trouble.

'I told you not to bring that ball,' Dough Boy says in disgust.

Ricky hesitates, but eventually he throws the ball. The gangster catches it and throws him a gang sign.

'Thanks, blood,' he says. He turns around to his friends. 'Yo Dog, catch.'

Mad Dog is six foot two in height, as wide as two Volkswagens, and looks as fearsome as his name suggests. He catches the ball in one hand and the gangsters begin throwing it back and forth.

Ricky looks desolate. Dough Boy berates him for being so stupid as to bring the ball. Tre tries to lead the group away but Dough Boy turns back and walks towards the older boys.

'Hey, gimme back my brother's ball!' he shouts.

'Dough,' Chris says urgently. 'Don't say nothing, they might give it back. I know them, they just playing.'

The first gangster turns to look at Dough Boy.

'What you say, fat boy? Nigga looks like the Michelin man.'

The older boys laugh, but Dough Boy doesn't shift.

'I said give my brother's ball back before . . . '

'Before what? What your fat ass gonna do?'

Dough Boy doesn't answer. Instead he charges the older kid, trying to pull the ball out of his hands.

Mad Dog watches, a strange look of sympathy on his face.

'Yo Rock,' Mad Dog calls. 'Give dat little nigga dat ball back.'

Rock takes no notice, and Ricky and Tre join in trying to get the ball, which he is holding high above their reach in the air. Dough Boy gets frustrated and kicks him in the knee. Suddenly the older boy's mood changes from amusement to anger and he kicks Dough Boy hard in the stomach. Dough Boy goes down and Rock kicks him again. Tre and Ricky, shocked, bend over Dough Boy, shielding him.

'Stupid muthafucka,' Rock grumbles. 'I was going to give it to you too.'

He turns his back on the boys and goes on with the game. They help Dough Boy to his feet and stumble off. Dough Boy holds his stomach, trying to keep the tears from flowing.

'Hey man,' Tre says, 'I gotta football. I don't ever use it much though. Tell you what, it's yours, soon as we get back.'

'He ain't going to want it,' Dough Boy says. 'His Daddy gave him that ball. I wish I could kill that muthafucka.'

As they go Ricky stares at the older boys playing with his football. As he watches Mad Dog catches it and looks in their direction. He pauses for a moment and their eyes meet. Suddenly, when it looks as

41

though he'll give it back Mad Dog turns to his homeboys and throws the ball. Sadly the three friends turn
to walk away. But they haven't gone very far when
Mad Dog calls out.

'Hey. Little man. Catch.'

He throws the ball and Ricky stretches his arms
out for it, a look of sheer bliss on his face. But it hits
him in the chest and bounces on the ground. Tre
runs to fetch it, and Dough Boy, still angry, makes
a face of disgust.

'Man,' he says. 'You're sorry.'

But Ricky is looking at Mad Dog and he nods a
thank you to the man who simply gives a faint smile
and turns away.

CHAPTER THREE

A hot, bright day in South Central L.A. The street is dry and dusty, lined with Spanish-style stucco dwellings. The music is hard to locate because it's playing in the open air and as it echoes round the neighbourhood it seems to be coming from every direction. Half-way down the street it settles down and you can figure out that it's coming from Mrs Baker's home, where there's a barbecue party going on.

The backyard is full of people, almost all of them young, all of them black. They're dancing underneath a banner which reads WELCOME BACK DOUGH BOY. In one corner a group of young men are playing a loud game of dominoes. Across the yard from them, in another corner, a large young man in a Washington High School football jersey is labouring over a sizzling barbecue pit. He has an open, friendly face, and he moves with the easy confidence of an athlete. From time to time he glances round smiling and his gaze focuses on Little Ricky, his two-year-old son, who he can see through the open back door, playing with a toy model of a police car. Eventually one of the women stops beside the boy. She looks over at Ricky by the barbecue pit and smiles back at him.

'Go on, Lil Ricky,' she says. 'You better go outside. Your daddy wants you.'

Little Ricky looks up in curiosity, then he gets up and walks in the direction of the backyard. As he goes he accidentally steps on the police car. Ricky grins at him.

'Come here,' he shouts.

Little Ricky walks across to his father who picks him up, hugs him and, without missing a beat, continues to poke and turn the meat as it cooks. He holds Ricky effortlessly in the crook of one arm and talks tenderly to him.

'C'mere,' he says. 'What you doing, huh? You want to learn how to barbecue?'

While Ricky is doing this Mrs Baker comes up to him, takes the fork out his hand and begins poking at the meat. She's his mother, but you have to look twice before you're certain that she's old enough to have such a big son. She's a slim, good-looking woman in her thirties, with a snap and a sway about her movements which can still turn a man's head. Ricky is seventeen, but like a lot of mothers she hasn't yet adjusted to the fact that her boys are teenagers, almost grown men, and she scolds them and orders them around as if they were still ten years old.

'Ricky,' she shouts. 'You not watching this meat. All you doing is poking at it.'

Ricky grins at her. By now he hardly notices her shouting, and his attention is fixed on a young woman also about seventeen who comes up and offers to take Little Ricky in her arms. She has a cheap perm and she's wearing biker shorts which show off every inch of her firm body. This is Shanice, the baby's mother and Ricky's girlfriend.

'I'll take him,' she says, but Ricky hugs his son tight and shrugs her off.

'Naw Shanice,' he says. 'I got him. Go on back to talking to your friends.'

Squeezed up behind the barbecue pit Mrs Baker keeps one eye on the young couple and the other on the meat. She loves Ricky passionately, and all her hopes for the future are focused on him. She's known Shanice her entire life too, growing up in the neighbourhood, but she has a cynical understanding of the young woman and she watches their relationship carefully.

'Ricky,' Shanice says. 'I got to check his diaper.'

Ricky turns his son over to smell his pants.

'He ain't wet. So go on. Go on, I got em.'

He shoos her away with his free hand, then he changes his mind.

45

'Wait a minute, c'mere.'

Shanice turns back, already knowing what he wants, and puts her arms round his neck. Ricky kisses her long and slow. Delicious. Behind them Mrs Baker, stewing in the heat between the pit and the fence, loses patience.

'That's how y'all got that one,' she shouts, coming round the pit and shoving them aside. 'Make sure she taking them pills, I don't want a whole stack o' babies running around here. I'll be the only one taking care of them.'

Ricky grins at her, untroubled. He's heard this before. But now Mrs Baker has got this off her chest, she cuts her eye across the yard to where her younger son, Darin, is seated, with three of his friends. Darin is trouble. Everyone calls him Dough Boy because he's always been overweight and oversize, but now his bulk looks tough and muscular, while his face has hardened into a challenging stare. Only Mrs Baker can still see the chubby kid he once was. For the last seven years Dough Boy has been in and out of the state's juvenile facilities, and the party is in celebration of his latest return from the pen.

Dough Boy's three friends are boys he's known for ever. They've grown up together in the street and together they've become South Central L.A. gangsters, gangbangers, soldiers in the neighbourhood wars. But to each other they're boyhood friends, Chris, Monster, Dooky, and Dough Boy, and at this moment they're just carefree kids, playing a ruthless game of dominoes. Judging by the passion with which they follow the game you'd think that money is involved. They smack their pieces on to the table making a loud, sharp bang every time, and they shout with delight at every successful move. Dough Boy is winning this time, and he slams the final piece down in triumph.

'Domino muthafucka,' he says. 'What you say to that nigga? What you say to that?'

Monster is a big, lumbering, ugly boy, who only feels really relaxed in this crowd. He gives Dough Boy a look of mock contempt.

'Fool, that ain't shit. I still beat your ass three times already. That's just one time, nigga. Let's play again.'

'Naw, I don't want to play again,' Dough Boy says. He's out of practice and he doesn't want to be beaten again, especially by Monster. 'Let's bust some spades.'

He opens a deck of cards and begins dealing them. Chris and Monster watch the cards, but Dooky's mind is far away. His hair is curled up in the big dooky-shaped braids which give him his nickname, and his attention is fixed on the group of girls sitting over by the house across the backyard.

'I want to get with one of the hoochies over there,' Dooky says.

There are about ten of them, round about sixteen or seventeen years old. T-shirts, biker shorts, Truk jewellery, their nails carefully manicured and polished. They are a collection of honeys, conscious of the boys staring across the yard and giving them back a cool display of what they're missing. Take a good look.

Shanice takes it with the dignified amusement of a lady who's settled and out of the game, and only one of the girls fidgets and looks uneasy, trying to avoid the stares. This is Brandi, a striking drop-dead fine babe, who turns her body away and faces the other side of the yard where some of Ricky's athlete friends are flexing their muscles and talking football scores.

Dough Boy catches Dooky staring straight at Brandi and he sneers.

'Dooky, you fulla shit!' he says loudly. 'Nigga, ain't no bitch gonna give yo ugly ass no pussy.'

'Nigga, I bet I get more pussy than you,' Dooky replies.

'Yeah, muthafucka you be getting that dopehead pussy. I get more pussy than you get air. Wit yo Wannabee Mack Daddy ass.'

'Who are you calling Wannabee Mack Daddy?' Dooky demands angrily. To him this is a real insult, because as far as he's concerned he's a genuine Mack

Daddy, a man who can get some pussy whenever he wants.

'You, nigga! No-pussy-getting muthafucka!' Dough Boy says triumphantly. 'Be fucking them dopeheads, stupid nigga.'

Dooky looks a little guilty at this, and his eyes shift around slyly. He's been warned enough times not to mess with diseased dopehead pussy.

'Nigga, you don't know what I be getting. I don't be fucking no dopeheads. I might let them suck my dick but I don't be fucking em. Shit . . . they got AIDS and shit.'

'Stupid muthafucka,' Monster says. 'Don't you know you can get that shit from letting them suck your dick too?'

At this, Dough Boy gives Chris a look of resignation. All the facts in the world won't change him.

'Thank you,' he tells Monster.

'Yeah, right,' Chris says, thinking furiously about the dopehead who'd sucked his dick the night before and wondering whether she'd given it to him. He shifted cautiously in his chair, testing the feeling in his groin.

'You a mark,' Dough Boy says contemptuously.

Dooky thinks for a moment.

'Well I ain't sick. I ain't all skinny and shit.'

Chris has been following the conversation with a grin, relishing Dooky's embarrassment.

'Whatch you mean, you ain't skinny?' he shouts, laughing. 'You so skinny you can hula hoop through a cherrio! And fool, you don't have to be sick. You could die five years from now from that shit.'

Dooky is taken aback. He's really worried now.

'Y'all trying to scare me.'

He looks around trying to figure whether this has got a response, but all they were giving him was blank looks.

'Can you really get it from letting them suck your dick?' he continues anxiously.

Dough Boy lets him sweat, looks at him poker faced, picks up his beer bottle, and takes a long swig. He puts it down, makes a show of shifting it away from Dooky's end of the table, then turns his attention to the cards.

'Just keep your ass back,' he advises Dooky, who is still staring at him anxiously. 'And don't be asking to drink out of the same bottle.'

Before Dooky can think of a reply, a movement at the patio doorway catches Dough Boy's eye, and he looks up to see Tre.

Tre has paused in the doorway for a moment, partly because he's aware of creating an effect, partly to check where everyone is. He sees Ricky, his best friend first, and they nod hello to each other. Little Ricky, struggling in his father's arms, waves awkwardly. Ricky holds Tre's glance and signals with his eyes towards the group of girls, who have seen Tre and are reacting by whispering to each other. No surprise. Tre is wearing smooth black slacks and a fashionable black shirt. His haircut is smooth too, with several mosaic lines running through it. No doubt. The brother looks sharp.

Brandi, sitting with the other girls, is hardly conscious of what they're saying. She's waiting for the moment when Tre sees her, and as their eyes meet and he smiles she almost gasps with tension. Outwardly she is cool and Tre can't tell what she's feeling. He's trying to read her expression, though, when Mrs Baker comes up behind him, spins him round and gives him a hug.

'Tre!' she says. 'How you doing sugar?'

'Just fine, m'am.'

Mrs Baker smiles fondly at Tre. She loves his polite manners, and with his ambitious attitude and stylish ways, she's always thought him just the right sort of friend for Ricky. Besides which, she's got a lot of respect and a soft spot for his father, Furious.

'That's good,' she says giving him an extra squeeze. 'The food will be ready in a moment. I'm going inside to bring out the rest of the stuff. Potato salad and things like that. Go on, everybody's here.'

She comes close to Tre again and her gaze flicks over at Dough Boy who is watching impassively.

'Go talk to Darin. Talk to him seriously. Maybe something you got will rub off on him.'

For a moment Tre feels like telling her that it's not so easy. Dough Boy's way of life started long ago. Instead, he simply nods his assent and starts over to the gangsters' table. As he approaches they acknowledge him with raised hands and fists, and Dough Boy gets up to give him a grip and a hug. As he hugs Dough Boy Tre's mind goes back to the first days he'd come to live in the neighbourhood. In those days it had been Dough who'd first come forward to play with him, and they'd soon become best friends. A lot had changed since then, but those memories were in the background to everything he felt now about Dough Boy, and he knew that this was something which would never change.

Dough Boy sits down again after greeting Tre.

'What's up, Mack Daddy?' Dough Boy says. 'I heard you was like Mr GQ smooth now. You working over at the Fox Hills Mall?'

'Yeah, I get a discount on clothes and shit,' Tre replies. 'You like?'

Dough Boy looks at him appraisingly.

'You look like you sell rocks.'

'Tre, you be pumping that rock?' Chris says.

'Hell naw, I don't be doing that shit.'

'You can't anyway, your daddy'd kick your ass,' says Dough Boy. 'How's he doing?'

There is a pause. Tre is still nodding 'Hello' to several people. Dough Boy keeps the air moving by continuing the conversation.

'I guess you heard I'm outta the pen now. I'ma try to stay out this time though.'

'That's what we're here to celebrate, right, man? How'd you get so big?' Tre asks, looking more closely.

'Working out, nigga. What else you think there is to do in there? I was pumping that iron at least three times a day. Rest of the time I spent reading or writing to one of my girls.'

'Reading?' says Monster.

Dough Boy reacts to the question with irritation.

'Yeah, muthafucka! I ain't no criminal. I know how to read. Shit.'

'Yo, what's Brandi doing here? Her mother letting her out the house now or what?' Tre says, changing the subject.

'She your bitch, you know more'n I know,' Dough Boy replies coolly.

'Mmmm, mmm, Lord help me. You still on that, Tre?' Chris puts in.

As he says that all of them look in the direction the girls are sitting. Shanice is telling her friends about Tre and his friendship with the Baker brothers.

'Girl, he's fine,' one of them, Shalika, says. 'I'd like to rush that. He go to Washington?'

53

Shanice tells her yes, glancing over at Brandi to see her reaction.

Another of her friends, Rene, jumps in.

'Oh, I seen him before. He works at the Fox Hills Mall.'

'Does he have a girlfriend?' Shalika asks, licking her lips.

Brandi speaks for the first time.

'Yes,' she says, with emphasis and challenge.

The two girls look over at her as if she'd appeared in a puff of smoke and eventually Shalika laughs, making a big production of it.

'He's cute anyway,' she says. 'You better keep his ass before somebody steals him.'

Before Brandi can reply Mrs Baker calls out that the food is ready. She and Ricky unload a pile of ribs into a pan. Everybody comes in force. Tre, Dough Boy, and the other guys move swiftly, but when Chris pushes back the table it becomes apparent that the chair he was sitting in is actually a wheelchair. This is the legacy of a shooting. Chris is a casualty of a skirmish in the neighbourhood wars, and he has permanently lost the use of his legs.

The group of boys surround the food and it looks as if the girls will be left out when Tre does a double-take, taps Dough Boy on the shoulder and gives him a poker-faced look.

'Hey,' Tre says. 'Why don't y'all act like gentle-men and let these ladies eat first?'

Dough Boy, already with a plate in his hand, cat-ches on right away. Mimicking Tre's manner, he gives his tray to the nearest female.

'Yeah, y'all act like y'all ain't never had no barbe-cue before. Let these ladies eat.'

He pauses.

'Hoes gotta eat too.'

The boys laugh and the girls are outraged.

'Wait a minute,' Shalika screeches angrily. 'Who you calling a hoe? I ain't no hoe.'

'Ooops. Oh, that's right,' Dough Boy says con-tritely. 'I'm sorry, bitch.'

Mrs Baker gives Dough Boy a look of warning.

Tre looks on as the crowd parts and the boys begin helping the girls to ribs. He's pointing in the wrong direction so he doesn't see Brandi till she touches him on the shoulder and he turns round.

'Hi,' he says lamely.

'Why ain't you called me in five days?' she asks him.

'Just a second,' he says.

He goes over to Ricky, leaving her hanging.

'What's up? Looks like she wants to talk with you.'

'I know. I'm taking my time.'

'Oh. So you're trying to run that game, huh?'

Behind him Ricky can see Brandi getting up and saying goodbye to his mother. She is leaving.

'Yeah,' Tre says. 'How am I doing?'

'OK,' Ricky tells him. 'But just one thing.'

'What?'

'She left.'

Tre gives him a crazy look. His cool play has failed. He doesn't stay long at the party after this, and in a while he's walking back home, a plate of food from the barbecue in his hand. His head is so full of Brandi and the problem of her attitude that at first he doesn't see the two-year-old walking unsteadily down the street. Then he sees the cars slowing down and he rushes out into the street to pick the baby up. He ignores the cars honking, goes towards the house opposite, and knocks loudly.

The woman who answers is thin and emaciated, a crack addict, pipe in hand. She is Sheryl, a neighbourhood dopehead. Tre knows her and he knows that she'll sell everything she owns, including herself, for a taste of rock, a strawberry.

'Why don't you watch your baby,' Tre says. 'She gonna get hit one of these days.'

Sheryl takes the baby with a dazed look on her face. She looks at Tre with interest.

'You got some blow? I'll suck it.'

Tre looks at her with disgust.

'Just keep her out the street. And change her diaper. Girl almost smell worse than you.'

He walks away shaking his head, and at first he doesn't notice the car that has stopped in front of him. It is a 1991 red Hyundai with dark-tinted windows, which stops, then cruises past Tre, moving very slowly, slower than walking pace.

Slowly the window opens and Tre sees Ferris, a man about ten years older, his hair done in a jeri curl and with a face tight and hard as a clenched fist. Tre knows him, and he knows he's a drive-by shooter who hangs with the neighbourhood gangsters. Suddenly Ferris moves and the barrel of a twelve-gauge shot-gun appears. He points it straight at Tre, who stands still, staring back at him. Time stands still. The thoughts rush through Tre's head. Foremost is the hope that Ferris isn't in the mood to shoot him. The man seems to know what he's thinking and he smiles cruelly, then pulls the shot-gun back, and makes a gang sign.

'What's up, blood?' he says, laughing.

Immediately the car takes off, screeches down the street and out of sight, the laughter of the gangsters inside it floating back to Tre.

Tre stands there for a moment, breathing hard to regain his composure, then he walks away towards his house. He's used to this. Gangsters had fun scaring people, when they weren't going to shoot them.

But you never knew which it was going to be.

CHAPTER FOUR

Back in the house Tre's father, Furious, is at the kitchen table writing cheques for the bills. Tre puts the plate down in front of him, and Furious starts on the food. When he's finished Tre asks him to trim his hair.

In a while Furious is working over Tre's haircut, his scissors clicking busily, clumps of hair falling away as he concentrates on the cutting.

Tre relaxes. Furious has done this for him more times than he can remember, starting with that first day he'd come to live here. Afterwards they'd gone fishing down on Palos Verdes Peninsula. Tre had been making sandwiches from the groceries they'd bought, when Furious asked him the question he always did.

'Are you a follower or a leader? A lion or a sheep?'

'I'm a leader.'

'What have I always told you?'

Tre thought for a moment.

'Always comb my hair, wipe my nose, and zip my zipper before I leave the house?'

Furious smiled.

'Beside that. What three things do I always say to you? Think before you answer.'

Tre thought about it, but he knew the answer.

'Oh, I got it. Always look a person in the eyes. You do that they'll respect you better. Two, you told me never be afraid to ask you for anything. Stealing isn't necessary. And the last one I think was to never respect anybody who doesn't respect you back. That right?'

'Yeah. You got it.'

There was a pause, while Furious considered the next thing about which he meant to talk to Tre.

'What you know about sex?'

Tre gave him a sheepish grin.

'I know I take a girl, stick my thing in her, and nine months later a baby comes out.'

Furious laughed.

'You think that's it?'

'Basically, yeah.'

Furious shook his head.

'Always remember this. Any fool with a dick can make a baby but only a real man can take care of his children.'

Tre nodded in agreement, and Furious continued thoughtfully.

'When your mother was pregnant with you I was seventeen. All my friends were dropping out of school, hanging out in front the liquor store getting drunk, or stealing. Some of them were even killing people. My friend Marcus got into robbing people and he wanted me to do it with him but I was, like, naw man, I got a son on the way. I knew you were gonna be a boy. So anyway, I wanted to be somebody you could look up to. That's why I went to Vietnam.'

He paused.

'Don't ever go into the Army. A Black man don't have any place in there.'

Tre listened. He understood most of what Furious was saying, but what mattered was that his father was talking to him, and sharing his thoughts. That was what he remembered about the day.

Later on in the car Furious got serious again.

'The reason I tell you all I do,' he said, 'is because when I was coming up I didn't have my father around to tell me things. Your grandmomma could teach me how to be independent but she couldn't teach me how to be a man. I had to learn a lot of things on my own.'

Thinking back Tre remembered the look on his father's face when he said that. It was all part of the day, and he remembered it too, because just after that conversation they'd come round the corner to see Dough Boy and Chris being taken away in a police car, its red and blue lights flashing, like a warning sign. Tre knew immediately what had happened. They'd been stealing from the store and got caught.

'Damn,' Furious had said, banging his hand on the steering wheel. 'Damn.'

The memory had faded but sometimes, at moments like this one, with Furious fussing round his hair, he remembers how it had been when he first came to live in the neighbourhood. He sneaks a look at his father from the corner of his eye.

'You getting old,' he says.

'You know I'm only seventeen years older than you,' Furious says indignantly. 'Some of your friends got daddies in their forties and fifties, big old sloppy cats with pot bellies.'

'You'll be like that some day. Big, old, fat, juicy, rolling belly, sitting in a rockingchair, and reading the funny papers and stuff. Then my kids, your grandchildren, they'll be running all around you talking about grandaddy, grandaddy, gimme a dollar, gimme a dollar.'

'You think so huh?' says Furious laughing.

Suddenly something strikes him.

'Wait, wait, wait, what's all this talk about grandchildren?'

'Whatch you mean?'

Furious presses him.

'You using those rubbers I gave you? I ain't ready to be a grandaddy yet,' he says.

Tre walks away, fending him off.

'Aw pops, why you sweating me? Don't worry, I can take care of myself.'

Furious gazes at him, sniffing. He's trying to figure out whether or not Tre is still a virgin.

'Have you had pussy yet?' he says bluntly.

Tre, confused, tells him the first thing that comes into his head. The truth is that he is a virgin, but somehow, he can't admit it to his father. His friend Ricky is already a father, and Tre has a suspicion that he is the only boy his age in the neighbourhood who still hasn't done the wild thing.

'What?' he says, then, 'Yeah, I have.'

After that there was nothing for it but to lie. The story is the fantasy that he has been working on at bedtime. It starts with Tre cooling on Crenshaw Boulevard when a babe driving a VW Rabbit rolls up.

Her name is Tisha, and she has a body right out of a *Jet* centrefold. All the guys are rushing her but she comes straight for Tre and gives him her number. As the tale goes on he gets to her house on a Sunday morning just after her grandmother and her mother leave for church. They get to it immediately he walks in the door. Tre carries her off to her bedroom and they do the wild thing. The story ends with Tre escaping out of the girl's window to escape her grandmother who's returned unexpectedly from church. It's a typical teenage sex fantasy but Furious doesn't spot this, and it doesn't occur to him that Tre is lying.

'What did you use?' Furious asks, frowning. His concern has grown as Tre tells his story.

'I used the same number she gave me.'

'No,' Furious says angrily. 'I mean what did you use?'

'Aw, man, why you sweating me? I didn't have to use nuthin. She said she was on the pill.'

Furious bows his head. He has a hollow, cold feeling in his stomach at the thought of Tre having unprotected sex with a strange girl he picked up on Crenshaw. Behind it is the thought that Tre has grown up, almost beyond the reach of his protection and guidance.

'Didn't I tell you,' he says, 'even if a girl says she's on the pill, to use something anyway? A pill won't keep your dick from falling off! Oh shit, what the hell. You'll learn. Why do you always like learning the hard way?'

Furious can't contain himself and he gets up to walk away. Then he turns back to Tre.

'I ain't ready to be no grandaddy. And clean up this hair.'

CHAPTER FIVE

Driving to school next day Tre is still thinking about the lie he'd told Furious and about his father's reaction. Ricky is beside him, relaxed as usual, eating his breakfast, a bacon and egg sandwich. He tells Tre that a recruiter from the University of Southern California is coming to see him. Tre nods.

'That's good.'

He knows that Ricky is trying for an athletic scholarship, but right now he can't concentrate on his friend's news.

'You know,' he says, 'I've never lied to my father. Well almost never.'

'Where's this coming from?'

'I lied to Pops yesterday, told him I weren't no virgin.'

Ricky looks puzzled.

'But you ain't. Is you?'

'Technically speaking I haven't. I mean I've sucked some titties and finger-banged a couple of hunnies but I've never stuck it in.'

Ricky gives Tre a long look, a piece of egg hanging from his lip. He licks it off.

'Why not?'

Tre looks at him sideways.

'You really want to know?'

'I asked, didn't I?'

'I was afraid.'

Ricky bursts into laughter.

'What you afraid of?'

'Of being a daddy.'

He looks straight at Ricky, who stops laughing.

'But I'm getting old, shit. Now that I want to flap some skins Brandi ain't down for it even if I wear a jimmy.'

Ricky doesn't answer. He is still brooding over what Tre has said. He loves his son but sometimes he worries about the responsibility, and what it means for their future scares him. Tre leans forward and turns on the radio. It is permanently tuned to Radio KDAY and he's just in time for King News.

CHAPTER SIX

It's an ordinary day in the neighbourhood. Dough Boy, Monster, Chris, and Dooky are sitting on Mrs Baker's porch drinking their lunch. A string of customers are arriving early, and they pass their money over furtively. In return the boys slip them a small package of rock. Sheryl, the strawberry, comes up the steps. She's clutching herself and trembling. Dooky gives her a look of disgust, but Dough Boy moves over genially like a friendly shopkeeper.

'Yo. Yo. What you need?'

Ricky is in the locker room at Crenshaw High preparing for a training session. His ankle is being taped up as he lies back on a bench. His magnificent body tenses and relaxes as he begins to pump himself up.

Back in the neighbourhood Dough Boy is standing on the porch. He's having fun, making a deal on his cellular phone. Beside him his friends are playing dice, laughing, shouting, and taunting each other the way they do with every game. A police car drives by slowly, the cops watching them intently. Everyone turns to look, and Dough Boy coolly drops a piece of rock cocaine on the ground and crushes it underfoot until it is a white smear.

'Fuck the police,' he says, his eyes hard.

Outside the school gates Ferris and a couple of knucklehead gangsters from the Hyundai club are loitering. Every time a girl goes by they try to pick her up. With no success.

Inside the school building Tre is immersed in the autobiography of Malcolm X, turning the pages eagerly as he finishes each one, and Ricky is putting on his shoulder pads, the muscles rippling in his broad back.

In front of Mrs Baker's house Dough Boy and company are cooling on the sidewalk. They don't see the dope addict creeping up on them until it's too late. He snatches Dooky's chain and runs for it, past Dough Boy and Monster, who react in a flash and start running him down. From his wheelchair Chris watches his friends catch the stumbling freak. They punch him till he falls and then begin kicking him on the ground. Dooky picks up a big trash can barrel and finishes the action by dumping down on the squirming victim.

★

Tre has finished his book and he walks down the school corridor. This is his familiar territory. A girl is having trouble with her locker and he goes to help. He opens it with ease and starts a conversation with her.

Out on the football field Ricky and three other players are running at speed towards a barrier with four cushions lining it. They hit the cushions hard, the brutal sound of the contact booming around the ground. The boys grunt loudly as they hit. 'HAH.'

In the street the homeboys are sitting on the wall watching for the honeys on their way home from school. Near them a few brothers are shooting craps, rolling the dice in their palms and calling out as they throw. A few Mexican girls, schoolbooks clutched tight, pass by the sidewalk on their way home. One of them catches Dough Boy's eye. She has deep flashing-black eyes and beautiful jet-black hair. He comes off the wall, staring at her as she goes by.

'Psst, hey you, hey you, psst. Hey, you, bonita, oooh you muy bonita chica,' Dough Boy chants in his best broken Spanish. 'You chica bonita. Come to my casa, let's do the loco thing.'

The girls glance at him sideways but they walk on. Then as Dough Boy turns to his friends the girl stops and moves back towards him. She smiles as she comes, and behind her the group of schoolgirls giggle in excitement.

'You got a phone number?' Dough Boy asks.

Back at Crenshaw High the school day has drawn to a close. Ricky is in the locker room taking off his jersey. He lies naked on the bench, a look of utter fatigue all over his face and his body. As the other players leave he doesn't bother to move.

It's an ordinary day.

South Central L.A.

CHAPTER SEVEN

Tre is driving home from school when he spots Brandi and her mother taking groceries into their home. Brandi, also on her way from school, is wearing her private-school uniform. Tre waves at them.

Brandi's mother waves back, happy to see him. Things have changed since he arrived in the neighbourhood. Now Tre has most of the qualities admired by the mothers in the street and Brandi's mother thinks she's been lucky that her daughter's chosen to be friends with the one kid in the street she'd have picked out herself. Furious, also, has earned a lot of respect in the street because of his care and devotion to Tre, and by now Brandi's mother has a definite soft spot for him.

Brandi takes no notice. Her feelings are more complicated. Her mother would be shocked, she thinks, if she only knew what her daughter and Tre mostly talked about lately.

Squeezing her lips tight shut she picks up a bag of the groceries and goes into the house, and when she comes out again Tre is standing by the car. Her mother loads him with two armfuls of groceries and he takes them in past Brandi.

'You didn't tell me Tre's going to Morehouse next year. How come you two don't talk any more? You used to be such good friends.'

If you only knew, Brandi thinks.

'I dunno,' she says. 'You should ask him.'

Tre comes out of the house and Brandi's mother sweet talks him a little more, gives him a message for Furious, and then goes in. Tre is just about to go when Brandi can't stand it any more.

'What's wrong with you?' she bursts out.

Tre looks away.

'Did somebody say something to me?'

'You heard me,' Brandi says furiously. 'Stop acting stupid and look at me.'

She can't contain her rage any more and she grabs him and begins hitting him.

Across the street Dough Boy and his friends sit up, a row of interested spectators.

'Why the silent treatment? You haven't talked to me for a week. I call and you tell your daddy to say you're not home. I call again you take the phone off the hook. What was so bad that you just stop talking to me?'

Both of them know what it is, but Tre has missed Brandi and he's been trying to provoke this crisis.

He's determined to make her talk about it, instead of just saying no.

'You know what it was. You gotta get with the program.'

Brandi sits down vigorously.

'I told you about that. I'm Catholic. It goes against my morals.'

Brandi must be one of the few girls he knew, Tre thinks, who had such strict morals. And he had to get hooked up with her.

Across the street the gang waits impatiently for the next move. It comes when Brandi gets up angrily and tries to march back into the house, but Tre stops her and they sit down again.

'Now, let me get this straight,' he says. 'You say you want to wait till you get married. I said I was gonna be the one who married you, so technically it don't make no difference whether we do it now or later, we're still gonna get married.'

Tre is bringing his analytical intelligence to the job of persuading her, but Brandi is too smart simply to be argued into anything.

'I want to go to college,' she says, 'before I get married, and there is no guarantee that I'm gonna marry you. Shoot, I don't even want no babies. You haven't even given me a ring.'

Tre shifts around uneasily.

'I'm not ready for all that yet.'

'But you're ready to act like we're married though, right?'

Tre has no answer to that. Instead he gazes off into the distance. He has tried everything now, and none of the techniques he's read about and experimented with seem to work on Brandi. If he had any sense, he thinks, he'd find himself a hootchie who was ready to give him what he wanted. But he knows that he won't. Brandi means too much to him. He turns to her.

'I missed you,' he says simply.

'I missed you too.'

They come closer and the movement ends in a long, passionate kiss.

On the porch opposite Dooky applauds the reunion, his eyes shining with delight. Dough Boy looks at him as if he's crazy. He's about to say something then he changes his mind and takes a drink of his forty-ounce bottle. But on the other side of the street a group of curious eight-year-olds riding past the front of Brandi's house have stopped to watch the show, and the sound of their laughter interrupts the lovers. The smallest of them is the boldest, and when Tre turns round in surprise he calls out.

'Y'all gonna do the hootchie-coo?'

Tre grabs a few pebbles and throws them at them and they run. But when he turns back from the street Brandi is on her way into the house.

CHAPTER EIGHT

That night Tre is on the telephone talking to Brandi when his mother calls. Furious is in the bathroom, shaving.

Tre is trying to persuade Brandi, as usual and as usual she is fending him off. Half-way through the conversation he calls out to Furious.

'Hey pop, Brandi's momma say you cute.'

Comes out of the bathroom, his face covered in shaving foam, ready to join in the fun.

'Ask her why she don't speak when I say hi.'

Tre relays this, then he breaks off.

I'm supposed to be talking to you not passing messages.'

He laughed.

'If my daddy mess with yo momma we might end up being brother and sister then we be doing incest. What? I'm just kidding.'

The signal light flashes on the telephone.

'Just a sec I got another call.'

He clicks over.

'Who dis? Hi momma. Just a sec I got Brandi on the other line.'

He clicks over, and his voice turns romantic again.

'So, baby. You gonna give me the skins or what?'

'Tre,' Reva's voice says reprovingly. 'This is your mother.'

'Ooops, I'm sorry momma. Just a sec.'

He clicks over, back to Brandi.

'Brandi, I gotta go.'

Sitting in her apartment in View Park Reva drums her fingers on the arm of the leather couch as she waits for Tre to come back to her. The house is furnished in leather, natural wood, and gleaming metal. Through the plate-glass window there is a broad view of the city, its lights shining and winking. Reva is a success, just as she'd planned, but sometimes she wonders whether the cost has been too high. When she took Tre to Furious's house, she didn't think about it as giving him up. But over the years they have grown apart, and she's lost the tight intimacy they shared when he was little. If she regrets anything, this is what it is. The phone clicks and she takes in a deep breath.

'Who this?' mimicking Tre. 'What kinda way is that to answer the phone?'

'Sorry momma,' he mumbles.

'Why didn't you come over this weekend?'

'I was cooling with Rick.'

Kenneth Brown as Little Chris, Donavan McCrary as Ricky (aged 10), Baha Jackson as Dough Boy (aged 10) and Desi Arnez Hines, II as Tre (aged 10)

Tre (aged 10) walks to school with his friends

▲ Dough Boy (aged 10), his mother, Mrs Baker (Tyra Ferrell) and Ricky (aged 10)

▶ Larry Fishburne as Furious Styles

◀ Tre (aged 10) and his father, Furious Styles (Larry Fishburne)

▲ Tre (Cuba Gooding, Jr.) with his father

◀ Dough Boy (Ice Cube), one of three close friends who grow up together in South Central Los Angeles, is living by the laws of the street

▼ Morris Chestnut as Ricky Baker

▲ (l. to r.) Tre, Furious Styles, and Dough Boy

◀ Tre and his girlfriend, Brandi (Nia Long)

▶ Tre clings to Brandi in despair over the seemingly endless violence in South Central Los Angeles

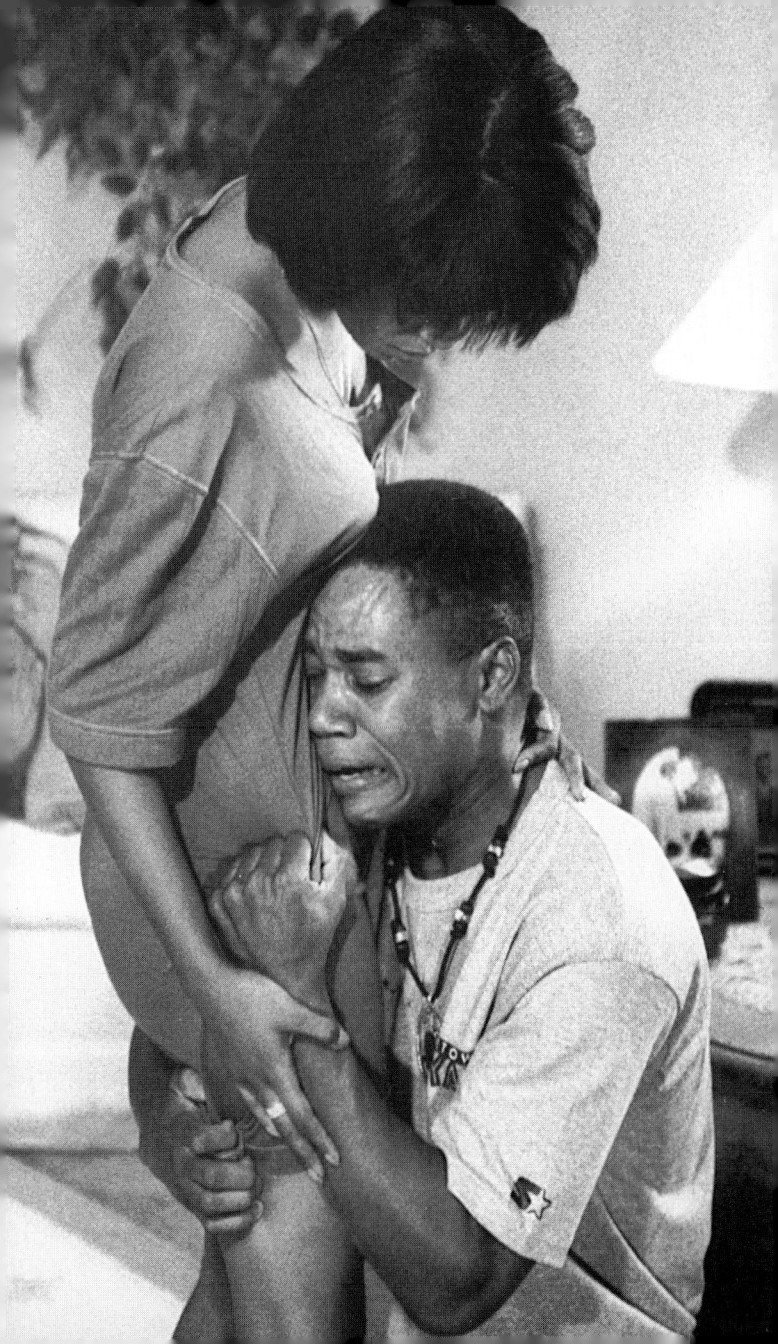

John Singleton, writer and director of 'Boyz N The Hood'

He had deliberately avoided going, but he couldn't tell her that.

'Well, you can cool with your friends any time,' Reva says, her voice taking on a faint undertone of upset. 'The weekends are supposed to be our time together. Have you thought about what we talked about?'

Tre knows that she'd ask. He'd been avoiding giving her an answer.

'Yeah. I dunno yet.'

'Let me speak to your father,' Reva says decisively.

Tre calls his father to the telephone and walks away, past him.

'Who dis?' Furious says, in exactly the same way as Tre had earlier.

Tre hears his side of the conversation as he walks down to his room.

'Oh, howya doing? We talked about that. Uh-huh, well, that's his decision. Personally I don't think it's necessary.'

Tre pauses at the door of his room, listening.

'You know this is some bullshit,' Furious says. 'There's no reason why Tre should stay with you now. He ain't a little boy any more. No, no, no. Why you got an attitude? Because what? I don't have an attitude, you got the attitude.'

Tre has heard enough. He's heard all this before anyway, and he closes his door, shutting himself off

77

from the sound of his parents arguing over him. Through the open window he can hear the sounds of the street. The flash of a helicopter spotlight goes past. For a moment Tre feels as if the neighbourhood is closing in on him, then he gets up and slams the window shut.

Across the street Dough Boy and his homeboys are coming out of the house. They'd been playing Nintendo and Monster had been shouting. 'Watch me shoot this muthafucka, look! Blam! Taken off the set!'

Dough Boy had warned him: 'Yo, Monster, don't be cussing so muthafuckin loud, my mother don't like that shit,' and criticized how he was sitting on the couch, saying, 'C'mon man, move the plastic, you're sitting on the good part,' but Mrs Baker had called him out of the room. 'See, now I gotta hear all this shit,' he'd complained.

'Man,' Chris had said in a wondering tone. 'Moms be fucking wit his ass without fail. She ain't like that with Rick though.'

Dooky nodded knowingly.

'They got different daddies, that's why.'

When Dough Boy came back he'd started shooing them out of the house immediately.

'Y'all gotta get the fuck out,' he'd said. 'My brother's having company in a little bit.'

Now they were moving on to the porch, looking forward to doing what they always did, drink, talk, and chill.

Around the corner creeps a late-model 1989 Nissan Sentra and it begins slowly cruising down the street. The boys are quick to notice. A car behaving like this could be a drive-by, almost certainly some kind of threat, and Dough Boy stands poised, watching it carefully. The window winds down.

'Anybody know where Ricky Baker lives?'

There's a pause while the boys adjust. Dough Boy is the first to react. Ricky's visitor, he guesses. The college recruiter from USC.

'That's my brother,' he shouts. There's a strange note of pride in his voice. 'He lives here.'

He turns to the doorway.

'Yo Rick, the man is here to see you.'

No one notices that Dough Boy is speaking grammatically, as he does whenever he wants to.

A Black man wearing horn-rimmed glasses, a neat business suit, and carrying a briefcase gets out of the car, and walks up to the steps where Dough Boy, Monster, Dooky, and Chris are sitting. As he comes, a helicopter sweeps overhead. The boys hardly notice but the man's eyes flicker upwards nervously. He's never lived in a neighbourhood like this, but he's heard about it on the news, drive-bys, gangbangers, bad boys like the ones facing him on this porch. The homeboys are regarding him with mild curiosity, he can't read their expressions and to his middle-class eyes they are the most intimidating sight he's seen so far. But he knows his job. Ricky is one of the best prospects he's seen this year, and he's determined to bring him to USC.

'What college you from?' Dooky asks.

'USC.'

'You gotta have a scholarship to go to USC?' This from Monster who's been thinking the whole business over.

Try making it without, the recruiter thinks, but he smiles.

'No, but it helps.'

'Hey yo. Can you get me a scholarship?' Monster says, making up his mind. 'I used to play baseball.'

Somewhere inside Monster a secret hope flickers dimly. He's a school dropout who once dreamed of being a professional athlete, or maybe playing ball at college. He knows there is no hope, but he has to ask.

The recruiter looks even more nervous, alarmed by Monster's persistence, but Dough Boy comes to his rescue.

'Why don't y'all move out the man's way? You see he's about the business. Move out da way, nigga.'

The homeboys fall back, frustrated, and Dough Boy ushers the recruiter into the house, where Mrs

Baker is waiting. The sight of her reassures him. She's dressed in her best, looking good and smiling sweetly at him. He stretches out his hand and introduces himself.

'Hello, I'm Lewis Crump. You must be Ricky's mother?'

He wonders whether to risk a compliment, but conscious of Dough Boy at his elbow, decides not to.

'Hi, my name's Brenda,' says Mrs Baker. 'This is my other son Darin. Would you like something? Coffee? Water?'

Dough Boy's face is a picture of amazement. But there's also something a little sullen about it. He's never seen his mother act like this before.

Ricky and Shanice come in and Crump smiles, pleased to see him. They begin talking football, Ricky confident and relaxed, Crump flattering him. Mrs Baker shoos Dough Boy and Shanice who are looking on with interest, and they all leave Ricky alone with Crump.

'Now,' the recruiter says, getting into his usual spiel. 'I just want you to know that we're interested in you coming to the campus, get a good look around. Ya know. A feel for the school as a whole.'

Ricky nods, but his attention is elsewhere. He picks up the remote control of the TV and clicks on a tape of recorded highlights from his best games.

The tape shows him running across the field and catching to the background of a cool bass rap beat. Crump has seen hundreds like this and he doesn't need it, but feigns being impressed. At the end he waits patiently while Ricky talks about his best game.

'What are you interested in,' he says suddenly, 'besides playing ball?'

Ricky has to think for a moment. It's the one question that throws him.

'What do you mean by that?'

'I mean,' says Crump, 'what would you want to major in? What kind of degree would you like to pursue? I'm just asking, because you know there's a strong possibility that you won't go into the NFL right after college. Just a fact. It happens.'

Crump has to say this. He's seen so many young brothers dumped at the end of a college career, injured, or not good enough, or fucked up with dope and bitterness. Ricky has heard about this, but his imagination doesn't stretch to the idea that it might happen to him. He thinks for a moment.

'Yeah, I heard that before,' he says putting on his serious face. 'Yeah well. I think I'd be interested in majoring in business. I got this friend named Tre who's always talking about going into business and all. Plus, I like computers, maybe I can do that. What do you think?'

Crump smiles.

'I think, young brother, you can do anything you put your mind to.'

This is Crump's job, but he's touched by the boy's honesty and naïvety. Rick isn't so sure about his capabilities outside of football and when he nods his agreement it is a nervous and uncertain gesture.

While Crump and Ricky talk, the homeboys on the porch are discussing college education.

'So I went up there, right?' Monster says. 'Cause my cousin had a class at this certain time and he said he'd show me around and 'duce to people ya know? So ya know, I get up there and there ain't nothing but women, hunnies as far as the eye can see. And all of them fine. Those that wasn't fine they had crazy boomin body! Big country bootie, big country titties! From eating all that cornbread and shit I guess.'

'Yeah,' Dooky says, his eyes shining. 'I'd go to college just to talk to them fine hunnies.'

'Fool,' Dough Boy breaks harshly into the dream. 'You don't go to college to be talking to no bitches. You supposed to be learning something. You can't learn nothing talking to no stupid bitches.'

They can't argue with Dough Boy, and Chris changes the subject.

'You know where you need to go, where they got more women than anywhere? Fine ones too?'

Everybody's got a different suggestion. Monster

says it's Crenshaw Boulevard on Sunday nights. Dough Boy comes up with the street races on Florence Avenue.

'Naw,' Chris says. 'Y'all way off. I give you a hint. Everybody's been there.'

'Where?' Dooky can hardly control his eagerness to know.

'Where?' Dough Boy shouts, losing patience. 'Where? Shit just come out wit it.'

Everybody looks at Chris, eagerly anticipating the name of this miraculous place where women abound.

'Da church,' Chris says triumphantly.

The homeboys explode with disbelief.

'Aw, shit, nigga, please,' Dough Boy says. 'Ain't nobody going to church to catch no bitches.'

'Naw, serious,' Chris replies earnestly. 'Listen. I went to church last Sunday, wasn't nothing but babes, full on biscuits straight, and I was one of the only men like around my age. And all these hunnies kept looking at me staring and shit.'

Dough Boy looks at him and shakes his head sadly.

'They probably was saying to themselves, where's this stupid muthafucka come from?'

The talk goes on. Tonight the homeboys are bubbling with exaggeration and argument. Inside the house, where the faint sound of their voices can be heard, Crump is winding up the business by checking

Ricky's qualifications and giving him some final instructions.

'So basically,' he says. 'You have a two point three Grade Point Average according to the classes we require. All you have to do is take the SAT test.'

A 2.3 GPA's not too bad, he thinks, low but average low. The Scholastic Aptitude Test was something else again. He eyes Ricky who is looking flustered.

'Yeah,' he says. 'I heard about that test.'

Everyone could take the test in their junior year, at sixteen or seventeen, and Ricky knew that the results could decide your future. Tre and Brandi had already taken it, got good scores, and would be trying again next time to improve on their results. But so far Ricky had managed to avoid having anything to do with it.

'The next one's being given in October. Are you going to take it?'

'Yeah, I guess so,' Ricky says, trying to look as if that had been his intention all along. 'Can't get into college without it. Right?'

Crump doesn't bother to reply to that.

'Just remember,' he says reassuringly. 'All you need to get is over a seven hundred.'

Most of his athletes could manage that with ease.

Suddenly Little Ricky runs into the room wearing a towel. He crosses in front of Crump and Ricky laughing and gabbling in baby language. Shanice follows close behind trying to chase her son down and at the same time trying to conceal her embarrassment.

'I'm trying to give him a bath,' she says laughing. 'C'mere.'

She grabs him and retreats smiling apologetically at the guest, but Crump has been charmed by the baby, and he turns, still smiling, to Ricky.

'Your little brother?'

'Naw,' says Ricky with careless pride. He's completely unaware of the effect his teenage fatherhood has on some people. 'That's my son.'

The smile wavers and leaves Crump's face.

'Oh.'

He sweeps his papers into the briefcase, snaps it shut, and rises in one smoothly practised movement. They say goodbye and Crump goes out quickly. As he canters down the steps Monster calls after him.

'Yo man. You gonna kick me down with a scholarship or what? I wanna go to college too.'

Dough Boy stands up.

'You man,' he says. 'Could you please shut the fuck up?'

Through the window he can see his mother come out of the kitchen and run to hug Ricky. She is bursting with pride and pleasure, and there are tears in her eyes. All of a sudden she has the feeling that it's all been worth it. Now she can be proud of her son the way Furious is with Tre. She holds Ricky close.

'My baby's going to a university,' she cries. 'I always knew you would be about something. When you were a little boy you used to run around all the time with that football under your arm. I'm proud of you.'

Over her shoulder Ricky's eyes are troubled, and when she lets him go he walks past her into the kitchen, grabbing a scrap of meat off the stove as he goes, then he walks slowly into his room. Mrs Baker stays in the middle of the room, her hands clasped together, transfixed with joy.

Through the window Dough Boy has watched the whole scene. There is a strange mixture of emotions going through him. Pride and gladness for Ricky, anger with his mother for showing out so clearly how much she loves his brother, when she's been treating him like a piece of shit his whole life, and behind all that is a kind of regret about himself. He's smarter than Ricky, he thinks, he's always known it. About as smart as Tre, only different. But his mother's about the only person around who doesn't know it. Thinking about that he watches her until she sits down on the sofa and throws her head back, smiling. Then he turns back to the homies.

'Let's get into something,' he says.

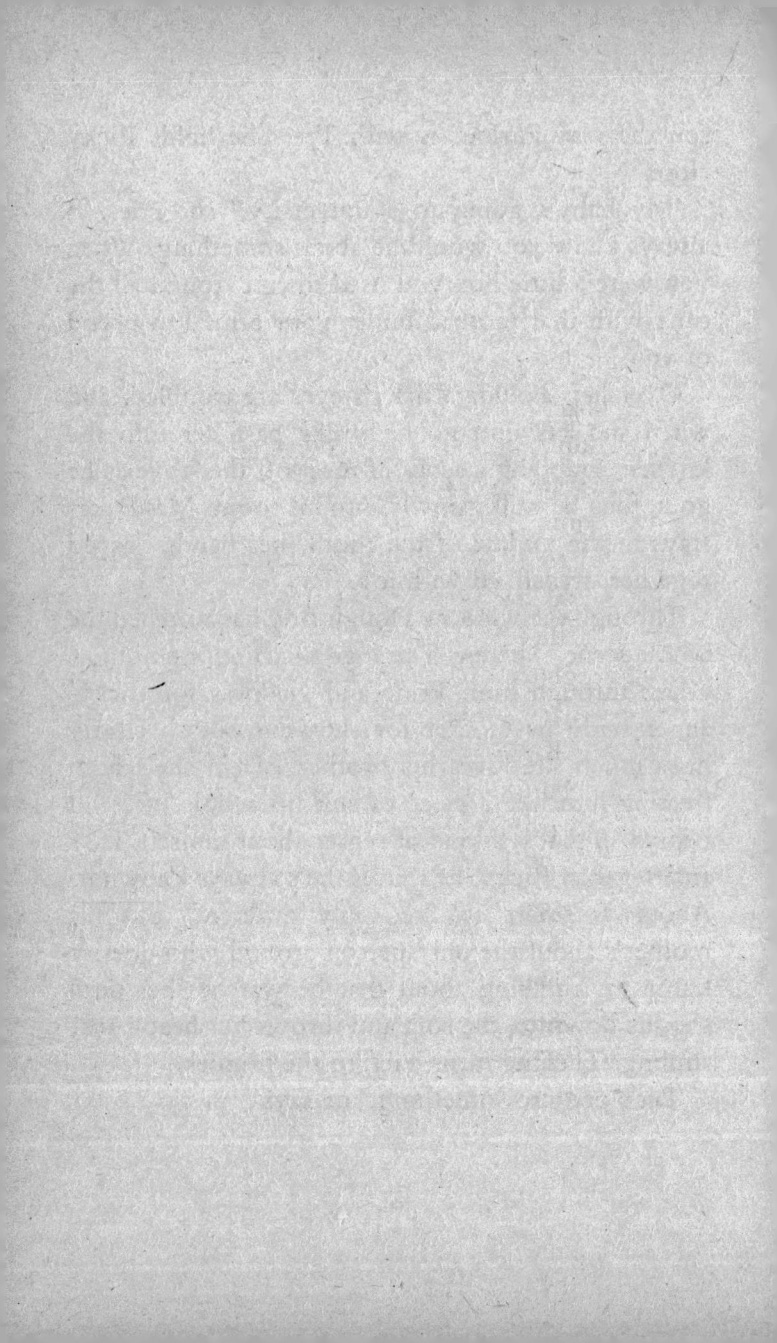

CHAPTER NINE

Thinking back to the night when he saw Crump, Ricky couldn't figure out where the time had gone. At first it seemed he had plenty of time, and he'd been determined to study as hard as he could. Tre had offered to coach him and he'd accepted gratefully. They'd become closer than ever, sitting together at the kitchen table in Furious's kitchen going through the kind of questions that might come up. Vocabulary, long division, fractions, percentages. Ricky had never worked so hard in his life. Sometimes Furious would come in, look at them sitting there, pat him on the shoulder and go into the living-room. Times like that he felt good, as if he was getting somewhere, but as the test got closer and closer, he could feel his mind going blank, the way it did whenever he had to do a test at school.

Now he's sitting in the classroom, waiting for the test to start. The room is full of Black students and all his friends are there. From where he's sitting he can see Tre, Brandi, and Shanice. At the front of the room a teacher is dictating the rules of the test. Ricky tries to listen as hard as he can.

'Please keep your test booklets closed,' the teacher says. 'You will have thirty minutes in which to complete each section of the test. Please stop when you are told to do so. You cannnot go back to a previous section after completing another.'

Tre looks over at Brandi, his eyes dreamy, to wish her good luck. Then he turns in Ricky's direction to do the same. Shanice and Brandi also signal luck to each other, with their eyes.

'You may now begin section one,' the teacher says.

This is the signal Ricky has been dreading. He opens his test book slowly, glancing towards his friends to see how they're doing. Each of them works at their answers differently, and you can tell something about each personality from the way they go about it. Tre is calm and steady. He does some rough work before circling a bubble. Brandi whisks away answers with ease, doing the calculations in her head, and she marks correct answers at a rate of one every ten seconds. Shanice is messy. She erases frequently, leaving a track of rubber bits on the paper which she blows away with her breath; then she looks around to see if anyone is watching her embarrassment.

Meanwhile Ricky is in big trouble. He's stuck on a question about percentages and he knows that he can do it, but somehow he can't get down to it. He puts his hand to his head as though this is giving him a headache, then he looks up from the test paper and out the window. He goes off into a dream, thinking about what Crump had said to him that night.

'I think you can do anything you put your mind to. All you need is a seven hundred.'

Tre stares at him, and he senses that he's being observed. When their eyes meet, Tre looks down at his paper, indicating that Ricky should do the same. Ricky nods and goes back to the test, but his eyes are depressed and frustrated. If I blow this, he thinks, it's my whole life.

CHAPTER TEN

The test is over and Tre is driving Ricky, Brandi, and Shanice home. Ricky is sitting in the back seat looking out of the window just the way he'd been doing during the test. For a while no one says a word until Tre breaks the silence.

'How do you think you did?'

'It was easy,' Brandi says. 'I had a book to study by.'

Tre ignores that. He's looking at Ricky's face in the rear-view mirror.

'Man,' Ricky says sullenly. 'Don't even ask me about that stupid test. All I want is a seven hundred. I don't care about nothing else.'

'I got a seven hundred last time I took it in the eleventh grade,' Shanice says cheekily.

Ricky throws her an angry look and she looks back defiantly. Tre and Brandi pick up Rick's anger and the tension it's causing but they say nothing. Minding their own business.

Tre stops in front of Brandi's house, and before she gets out she reminds him that they're meeting at

ten that night. Then she gives him a long goodbye
kiss, which gets longer and longer. Behind them
Rick rolls his eyes signalling that he thinks this is
dumb. But Shanice looks curiously at her two
friends, getting almost close enough to touch them
as they kiss.

'How come you don't kiss me no more?' she asks
Rick, her eyes challenging.

'I kiss you,' Ricky says. He doesn't want to get
into this especially with Shanice in the edgy mood
she's in.

'Yeah,' she says sarcastically. 'You kiss me when
you want some pussy. You act like an old married
man.'

At the moment that is just how Rick feels, but he
doesn't say it. Instead he takes her in his arms, bends
her backwards in a low dip and kisses her romanti-
cally. As he lets her go he can see she's softening up,
and he can't resist teasing her a little.

'See, and I don't even want no pussy right now.'

Shanice pats her hair. She's reassured, but isn't
going to let it go.

'Yeah,' she says. 'But you will.'

Brandi and Tre stop kissing at last, and Brandi gets
out, while Shanice stays where she is. The house is
just on the opposite side from where they're parked,
and when Ricky realizes that Shanice isn't getting out
he explodes.

'You can't walk across the street?'

Shanice has really been waiting for Ricky, but she knows now that he wants to be with Tre and she gets out. This is exactly what she meant about acting like an old married man, parking his wife at home and going disappearing with his friends, but she decides not to say anything yet.

'What time you gonna be home?' she asks.

On top of the way she'd been smartmouthing him earlier, the question seems designed to make him lose face in front of his friend, and he gets out angrily, climbs into the front seat, and slams the door.

'When I feel like it,' he throws at Shanice as he does this.

As Tre drives away Shanice walks slowly across the street to where Mrs Baker stands on the porch holding little Ricky. She gives a look of sympathy, but Shanice simply takes the baby from her, and holding him tight, goes on into the house.

A few minutes later Tre is driving towards Compton. He's taken the day off to do the test and now he's going to see Furious at his office. Beside Tre Ricky stretches and leans back. He's along for the ride. He peers out of the window.

'Man,' he says. 'I can't believe you ain't flap skins yet with Brandi.'

'She don't want to do nothing till we get married.'

He's still hoping, but now he can live with the situation.

'That's bullshit,' Ricky says emphatically. 'They all wanna bone. It's human. They just don't like admitting it to nobody except they girlfriends and all. You think you gaming on em and they the ones that gaming you. That's cool though. At least you know you ain't got no hootchie-momma on your hands.'

Tre nodded. He wasn't going to argue with a man of Ricky's experience about sex and women, but privately he figured that Brandi must be different.

Before long they're driving down Alondra Boulevard. They are near the airport and a light plane goes overhead. As Ricky stretches to see it, he notices the sign which reads WELCOME TO COMPTON. He looks at it apprehensively. 'Goddamn,' he says. 'Mary, Jesus Christ, we in muthafuckin Compton. My brother was seeing this biscuit out here and she almost got him shot.'

Tre reassures him and in a few minutes they're in front of Furious's office. It is a shop front with FURIOUS STYLES FINANCIAL SERVICES written across it in huge letters.

Furious is on the phone but he sees them come in and acknowledges their arrival. Then he puts down the phone and sits back in his chair. Here in his own office Furious has all the assurance of a king on his throne.

The first thing he asks is how they did in the tests, and when they both mumble 'all right', he tells them that most of their tests are culturally biased. Then:

'So what are you two knuckleheads doing out here?'

Furious is a mortgage broker and when Ricky asks about the business he begins explaining, then breaks off.

'You want to see something?'

In a few minutes they're driving through Compton in Furious's car. They stop on a corner in front of a vacant lot and Furious gets out.

'I don't know about this, Furious,' Ricky says nervously to Tre, 'got us walking in muthafuckin Compton and all.'

'This is the nineties. We can no longer be afraid of our own people,' says Furious. He leads them to the foot of a billboard on the lot. The sign across it offers CASH FOR YOUR HOME.

'Look up there,' Furious says. 'You know what that is? You know what that's called?'

Tre and Ricky look at each other at the same time and look back at Furious.

'A billboard.'

'No.' Furious says testily. 'What are y'all two? Amos and Andy? Are you Step and he Fetch? I mean what that message stands for. It's called gentri-fication.'

In the background people who are from the neigh-bourhood are drifting by and Furious's manner and his voice attract attention. A small crowd begins to gather behind Tre and Ricky, who look around amazed at the speed with which it happens. Furious is untroubled, and he carries on speaking in the same strong tones.

'It happens when the property values of a certain area are brought down so that the land can be bought at a lower price. Then they buy the land, move the people out, raise the property value, and sell it at a profit. We need to keep everything in our neighbour-hood Black. Black owned, with Black money, just like the Italians, the Koreans, the Mexicans, and the Jews do.'

By now the crowd around Furious is reacting. Most of the people are nodding their heads in agree-ment, except for one old man in the front. He has a sceptical look. He's heard all this before or read it in the Muslims' paper and he's gearing himself up for an argument.

'Ain't nobody outside bringing property values down,' he calls out, 'it's these people around here shooting each other, selling that crack rock and shit.'

Furious faces him.

'How do you think that crack comes here? We

don't own any ships, we don't own no planes. It's not us that are floating and flying that shit into the country. But all you see on TV is Black people selling crack. Pushing da rock. Pushing da rock. It didn't even become a problem until it started showing up in places like Iowa and Wall Street where there ain't no Black people. And if you wanna talk about guns . . . ' By now there is fire in Furious's voice, and he stands straight and proud. There are a few gangsters in the crowd and he meets their eyes firmly. 'Why is it there is a gun shop on every corner in this part of town? You don't see gun stores in no muthafuckin Beverly-a-fuck Hills. You don't see no liquor stores on every corner out there.' He pauses. 'I'll tell you why. Because they want us to kill each other off. What they couldn't do in slavery they are making us do to ourselves. The best way you can destroy a people is take away their ability to reproduce. Lemme ask you this. Who is getting killed out here every night? The men. Nothing but brothers.'

The gangsters look at each other. They're impressed by Furious's style and what he says is familiar. One of them shouts from the back of the crowd.

'So what am I supposed to do some fool roll up and try to smoke me? I'm gonna shoot that fool back if he don't kill me first.'

Furious looks at him with a resigned expression. Then he gathers himself to teach the brother a lesson.

'Can't you see? That's exactly what they want you to do. You gotta think about the future, my brother. Do you know that in twenty years people are estimating that the population of Black people in this country will decline? Not move up. But down. What you gotta do is think about what are you doing to prevent that from happening.'

CHAPTER ELEVEN

Driving back to the neighbourhood the boys are thoughtful, still hearing the echo of Furious's words and the way they had affected the people listening.

'My brother shoulda heard that,' Ricky says. 'Woulda done him some good.'

Tre nods.

'Where is he now?'

'Where else? Up on Crenshaw with the rest of those fools and their cars.'

But that's where they're going.

Crenshaw Boulevard is in its night-time party mode. Along both sides of the street are rows of cars, each row is a line-up of a distinct make and model of car. These are the Crenshaw car clubs. The Suzuki Samurai club, the Mustang 5.0 club, the V-Dub Club, the BMWs, the '64 Impala club. The cars gleam and sparkle, furnishing the street, like objects of art, rather than machines for the humble job of driving people around.

Outside the cars their owners can be seen hanging

out talking to the ladies who drive by in their own cars. People are coming and going continually, walking in groups and stopping to talk to their friends who are parked by the kerb. Above all the noise of voices and engines is the steady, pounding bass line of a rap sound.

Dough Boy is sitting high up at the wheel of his '64 Impala. Shalika is beside him, Chris and Dooky in the back.

Chris and Dooky are discussing religion.

'You believe in God?' Chris asks.

Dough Boy interrupts. 'Why in the fuck are you getting so damn religified lately?'

'Fool, I wasn't even talking to you! This is an A and B conversation and you can *see* your way out!'

'Yeah, you can see your way out my ride too, and we'll see your cripple ass walking all the way home,' he says.

'Oh, *you* wanta get real? Fuck you, nigga!'

'Do I believe in God?' Dooky says. 'Yeah, I guess I do. How else could we have things like stars and the moon and shit like that?'

'Sun, moon, stars, quasars, nigga sound like Elroy Jetson,' Dough Boy says. 'There ain't no God. If there was a God how come he lets muthafuckas get smoked every night? Babies and little kids and shit? Tell me that.'

Shalika breaks in.

102

'Well you tell me this. How do you know God is a he? He could be a she, you don't know that?'

'You don't know what the fuck I muthafuckin know. I read about that shit when I was in the pen. It was this book that was trying to take life and shit from the perspective of if God was a bitch. And it said if God was a bitch then we wouldn't have no nuclear bombs and shit, and there wouldn't be no wars and all, because that ain't a bitch's nature.'

'Why every time you talk about a female,' Shalika returns, 'you gotta say bitch, or hoe, or hootchie?'

'Cause that's what most females are,' Dough Boy says.

'Yeah,' Chris joins in encouraged by Shalika's rebellion, 'and how come you say muthafucka all the time? Every other word you say got muthafucka in it. I know I say it too but I started thinking bout what that means when I say it.'

Dough Boy makes a gesture.

'It don't mean shit, I'm just trying to get my point across.'

'Still you shouldn't say it.'

Dooky joins in the chorus of disapproval and Dough Boy turns to look at him, eyebrows raised.

'Who are you now, Reverend Ike? Shut up, muthafucka, before all y'all asses be walking home.'

Their arguments usually end this way, but Dough

Boy is relieved to see Tre and Ricky drive up. They get out and walk towards Dough Boy's car.

'Where y'all coming from?' he asks as they reach the Impala.

'Compton. What y'all doing.'

Dough Boy looks round ironically.

'We just sitting here philosophizing about God, Church, bitches, and all.'

Ricky and Tre are standing out beside the car, and just then a group of brothers in red pants and red satin jackets walk up the street in a group. Ferris is leading them and as they pass he brushes up against Ricky. Ricky stares after him indignantly and Ferris, catching his attitude out of the corner of his eye, turns round to look back at him.

'What are you looking at, nigga?'

'I'm still trying to find out,' Ricky says.

Ferris isn't sure what his words mean, but he understands the tone and he moves towards Ricky aggressively. Immediately, some female members of the club try to intervene. But in the background all the members of the Impala club are jumping out of their cars and moving towards the action. Ricky and Ferris are staring at each other with stone-cold eyes, but Dough Boy looms up behind Ricky, his jacket pulled back to show his right hand gripping the butt of his gun. Ferris sees this and lets himself be pulled back into the crowd.

The Impala members relax.

'You see,' Dough Boy says philosophically. 'That's why fools be getting shot all the time. People trying to show how hard they is and shit. Ignorant.'

'Shut up fool,' Chris says. 'You be doing that shit too.'

'I know.'

Dough Boy laughs and turns to Chris, but suddenly there is a rapid burst of automatic fire. The street breaks into movement like a scurrying ant heap. People scatter for their cars, among them Tre and Ricky. Dough Boy pulls out his gun and starts his car up, and screeches off. Everywhere along the street people are running, cursing, shouting, crouched low, and gazing around for the source of the shots as they go.

Down the street Ferris grins in satisfaction at having broken up the party. He checks his gun and tosses it into his red Hyundai and then calmly gets in and drives away.

CHAPTER TWELVE

Tre and Ricky drive back home in silence. Coming on top of the tension they've been through that day, the incident has upset them.

'I'm getting the fuck outta L.A.,' Tre shouts suddenly. 'Fuck this shit, can't go nowhere without it getting shot up and shit. Damn.'

Ricky doesn't reply, but there is a blank worried stare on his face. Neither of them notice the police car creeping up behind them, until there is a sharp *whurr-whurr* of its siren.

Tre pulls over and a voice blasts out at them from the police loudspeaker.

'Don't move. Driver. Put your hands on the steering wheel. Passenger. Put your hands on the dashboard. Driver. Open the door with your right hand.'

The boys do as they're told and as they get out the cops come up behind them, guns drawn and pointed straight at them. Tre doesn't remember who they are until much later, but the pair are Coffey and Graham, still working the neighbourhood. Coffey's attitude is exactly what it was when he answered Furious's call, but the years in between have made him harder and more vicious.

'Keep your hands where I can see them.'

Tre and Ricky do exactly what they're told. In the back of their minds is the knowledge that this situation is even more dangerous than what happened on Crenshaw. Apart from drive-bys being stopped by the cops is one of the easiest ways a brother can get himself killed.

As the cops approach more police cars roll up, surrounding them like a pack of dogs round a piece of meat. Coffey and Graham push the boys up against the cars, kick their legs apart, and frisk them while the other cops begin searching the VW.

'Got any drugs or weapons on you?' Coffey snarls.

Tre looks at him out of the corner of his eye, paralysed with fear. Coffey puts his gun in the boy's face, close up under his nose, then Coffey moves closer, staring him right in the eyes, so he's forced to keep looking. In the cop's eyes he can see the shadow of a terrifying rage and madness, and somehow he knows that he is nearer death at this moment than he's ever been.

'You think you tough,' Coffey growls. 'You think you tough? Scared now, huh? I like that. That's why I took this job. You ain't shit. I hate little muthaf-uckas like you. Little niggas think you tough, huh? How you feel now, huh? I could blow your insides out with this Browning, you couldn't do shit. What set you from? You look like one of them Crenshaw Mafias muthafuckas. Naw. You probably a Rolling Sixty, huh?'

Tre doesn't move or even blink, and Coffey holds his position for a moment, as if making up his mind what to do. But by this time the cops have finished searching the car, and the police radio bursts into sound.

'Car 54, aah. Found that VW. 48 has them on Vermont and Florence. Need backup, officers are seeing resistance.'

The other cops run for their cars, and Coffey draws back. He steps back, and as he does so, sees that Tre has a tear in his eye. The sight gives him a strange thrill.

'Well, you gentlemen,' he says, deadpan. 'Have a nice day.'

It is past ten o'clock and Brandi, waiting for Tre, is sitting at the desk in her room, studying calculus, writing equations, the long rows of figures covering the paper rapidly. From time to time there are bursts of automatic fire and a couple of times when they're close, she drops her pencil in shock. Eventually she puts the pencil down in frustration. She can't concentrate. Her eyes pass over her desk, and dwell on a picture of herself and Tre. She wonders where he is, but she doesn't dare let herself think about where he might be. On the radio Greg Mack is matching up a couple in the KDAY love connection, and Brandi is just beginning to respond to the dreamy vibes when there is a knock on the door.

Slowly she gets up and goes over through the living-room to the front of the house. She hesitates and the knock comes again.

'Open up.' It is Tre's voice. 'It's me.'

Brandi begins opening the door. There are four deadlock bolts and it takes her a while. Then the door swings open to the steel guard door. Through the bars, Tre is looking at her impatiently.

'Boo,' he says. 'Open up. It ain't July out here y'know.'

Brandi opens the door and he comes in.

'You're late,' she says putting her arms round him. 'I thought something might have happened to you.'

'I'm all right. Nothing's gonna happen to me.'

At this moment Tre doesn't really believe that, but he wants to protect Brandi, keep the knowledge of what's happening out there from her.

'I'm tired of hearing them shooting all the time,' she says. 'I want to get out of L.A.'

Tre doesn't reply and suddenly Brandi notices the crazy look of rage in his eye.

'What's wrong?'

'Nuthin,' he says again. Then in the next moment

110

he loses his control and he can't hold the emotion back any more. He swings violently at the wall, shadow boxing round the room, hardly knowing what he's doing.

'I'm tired of this shit,' he shouts, transcendent, blazing with rage. 'I'm tired of this shit. Fuck this shit. I wish I could kill all these muthafuckas. Damn. I'm tired of this shit. Kill. Kill em all.'

Brandi sits back on the couch, shrinking a little. She's never seen this side of Tre before. But as he runs out of steam she gets up slowly and begins to approach him.

'Stupid muthafuckas,' Tre gasps. 'All of them. Need to die. All die.'

He begins to cry, slowly at first, then the tears start to flow heavily. Brandi puts her arms round him. She is crying too. But he pushes her away violently, ashamed to let her see him like this. Immediately he does so, though, he recovers himself and tells her he is sorry. They embrace again, and after a little while Tre starts laughing. Brandi laughs with him. Then she stops.

'What's so funny?'

'I never thought I'd cry in front of a female before,' Tre tells her.

'You can cry in front of me,' Brandi says tenderly.

They stay wrapped around each other, and in a minute she puts her hand down to stroke his behind.

'You need a booty,' she whispers. 'I gotta have something to hold on to.'

Tre can't believe what she's saying.

'I don't need no big ole butt,' he teases. 'That's supposed to be your job.' Then: 'Is your mother home?'

'No,' Brandi says. 'She woulda heard all that noise you made if she was.'

It's like a signal. In a flash they're in the bedroom where they fall on Brandi's bed kissing passionately. From here they can still hear the neighbourhood sounds, and from time to time the spotlight from a patrol helicopter glares through the window. Slowly the lovers undress. As Tre takes off Brandi's bra he bends over to kiss her breasts and she moans with delight.

'And I don't want to get pregnant,' she manages.

'You won't,' Tre says.

He's armed with a condom, and by the flashing lights of the helicopter beams coming through the window he puts it on. Then he moves between Brandi's legs, lowers himself into her, and gives a deep sigh of pleasure.

CHAPTER THIRTEEN

2.30 a.m. Tre is lying back in bed, wide awake. The last twenty hours have been the most eventful in his life, and he's too restless to sleep. He gets up, looks around, does a handstand against the growth chart on the wall, then goes to the closet where he pulls out an old box and takes out a projector. He gets out an old piece of film of himself and his mother holding him and playing with him as a baby and runs it through, looking carefully, although he knows it by heart. In the morning he'll be seeing his mother and his mind is focused on her.

'Go to bed,' Furious's voice says outside the door.

'Why didn't the two of you ever get married?' Tre says immediately.

Furious has been expecting the question. Sooner or later.

'Cause we loved each other too much.'

'But when you love somebody,' Tre says, 'you suppose to marry them.'

'Not always. There are people who think, act, and

live different. They love each other but they can't live together.'

He wonders if Tre understands. He shakes his head.

'Now go to sleep. You know how she is about being on time.'

Tre lies back, thinking about what Furious has said. He's already discussed what to do with Brandi, and this has made up his mind for him. As soon as school is out they're planning to drive South, and stay with her family while they look for jobs and an apartment, where they can live together while they're at college. She didn't want to get married and have a baby before she finished college, Brandi had said, but they could live together. Tre still couldn't get over the way she'd changed all of a sudden, from a reluctant schoolgirl to a woman planning and making decisions, but the plan sounded fine to him. He lay back thinking about how he would tell his mother that instead of coming to live with her, he'd be going straight off to college with Brandi. It's going to be difficult, he thinks.

Later on, sitting in Reva's house in View Park he knows that his guess was right. Reva didn't explode. That wasn't her way, but he could tell from the look in her eyes that she isn't going to accept this without an argument.

'You gonna live together?' she says incredulously.

114

'I don't think you should do that your first year. You should be married before you live together.'

'I was thinking about that too.'

'Tre. Once you get down there there's gonna be so many dirty party girls around that school you ain't gonna know what to do with yourself. You're only seventeen. You don't even need to be thinking about getting married. You need to see the world first.'

'What's wrong with me and her seeing the world together?' Tre asks.

'Do what you wanna do,' Reva says despairingly. 'I just don't want to see you dropping out of school having to take care of a baby and all.'

'You mean like you and Daddy?'

This is hitting below the belt, but Reva is affected by the comment and she thinks before she answers him.

'Yeah. Like me and your father. Things change when a baby comes into the picture. You call yourself loving this girl, so you better let her get her education. Yours also.'

Next day Reva is sitting in a chic café waiting patiently. Furious walks in. He looks around, taking in the atmosphere of the place before he sees Reva. It is rich. Furious crosses to where Reva's sitting and joins her. 'This is you, this is definitely you,' he says.

'What is that supposed to mean?' she says.

'I thought we were gonna talk about Tre?'

Just then a waiter interrupts him.

'Espresso please,' Reva says. Furious orders café au lait.

'I bought him some shoes yesterday,' Reva tells him.

'Quit buying him shit,' Furious says.

'Did he tell you he wants to move in with Brandi when they go to school?'

'So?'

'So? Don't you think it's a bad idea?'

The waiter arrives with their coffee and Furious says: 'Tre makes his own decisions.'

'You're his father, that means you're supposed to guide his decisions.'

Furious puts down his coffee cup. 'What the hell you think I been doing all these years? Listen, Reva, it's time to let go. I know you wanna play the mommy and all but Tre's a man now. He's not a little boy any more, that time has passed, you missed it.' He's finished, he gets up for some cigarettes.

'You're not getting off that easily. Sit your ass down.'

'What?'

'I said sit your ass down before I raise my voice and make a fool outta the both of us.'

Furious sits down coolly.

'Now this is my time to talk,' Reva begins. 'Of

116

course you took in your son, my son, our son, when I was trying to make something of myself, trying to better my life. You taught him what he needed to be a man. I'll give you that because most men aren't man enough to do what you did. But that gives you no reason, you hear me, *no* reason to tell me I can't be a mother to my son! What you did is no different from what mothers have been doing since the beginning of time. It's just too bad more brothers won't do the same. Don't think you're special!'

Listening to her Furious has been frowning but now he slowly lets it turn into a smile.

CHAPTER FOURTEEN

Dough Boy and his friends are at the start of a normal day on the porch. It's one of those days, everybody's feeling good at the same time. They're so busy talking and laughing that at first they don't notice a red 1991 Hyundai cruising slowly down the nearest cross street. But the second time it rolls up and stops the homeboys can't miss it. Everybody on the porch tenses up. They know Ferris's car and they know that there are drive-by shooters in it. Dough Boy stands and faces the Hyundai spreading his arms wide to show that his hands are empty and that he isn't packing. No one else moves. Anything can happen. Then, suddenly, Ferris stamps on the gas and the car screeches away up the street.

The boys on the porch ease up, and sit back laughing.

'That punk muthafucka,' Dough Boy says. 'Ain't got nothing better to do. Twenty-seven years old and still trying to hang out with niggas our age, with his old ass.'

'Yeah,' Chris agreed. 'I heard that fool been in da

pen so many times he had a nightmare and woke up with his arms behind his back like this.'

He shows them how.

'And that fool couldn't move his arms and shit.'

Tre arrives just in time to hear the end of this.

'What's up?'

Dough Boy's very interested to see him.

'Nothin much,' he says. He lowers his voice. 'The other night I saw yo ass rolling outta Brandi's crib about two in the muthafuckin morning. What's up wit dat?'

Tre grins. A satisfied little grin.

'That's my business,' he says.

'Uh huh.'

Dough Boy knows exactly what to make of that answer. His voice takes on a fatherly severity.

'Handle yo shit, man, handle yo shit. Don't end up like this fool in there. He got a baby, and in-house pussy.'

He glances back towards the house, with an aggrieved air.

'If I do that shit moms be like,' he does an impression of his mother, 'I ain't having it.'

In the living-room Ricky is sitting back on the couch watching a commercial for Army recruitment, which has come up in the middle of a football game. Shanice has been calling out to him to go down to the store and get her some corn meal so she can fry some fish. But Ricky takes no notice. He's watching the screen intently while a voice preaches over a series of images of young men running about carrying weapons, dropping out of helicopters, or typing computers. The images make the Army look like a brilliant career move for ambitious people, and they're well chosen to appeal to the young Blacks and Hispanics who fill the recruitment centres in poor neighbourhoods.

'Be all you can be,' the voice on TV rings out. 'Keep on living. Keep on growing, find your future, in the Army.'

The message gets to Ricky. Perhaps, he thinks, this will be one way of making sure that little Ricky has a future. Shanice calls out to him again, and Mrs Baker, disturbed by the noise, appears from her room.

'Ricky. Go get this girl some corn meal. You should be happy somebody's cooking for your ass. I ain't.'

'All right. All right,' Ricky says. 'I'm going. I'm going.'

He gets out and stumbles on to the porch.

'D,' he says to Dough Boy. 'Go to the store, man, and get some corn meal.'

Dough Boy has no intention of moving, and this is a good chance to tell Ricky some stuff he should hear.

'Nigga,' Dough Boy says. 'I ain't the one she asked to get it. That's your wife. You go get the shit.'

'She ain't my wife.'

'Shit,' Dough Boy says triumphantly, 'she might as well be your wife. You got a family and shit.'

Ricky decides to ignore him. He stretches and yawns and walks towards the steps, but as he goes he can't resist a comeback.

'Fuck you.'

Dough Boy has been itching to confront Ricky, and now he moves round and gets in front of him.

'Don't fuck me. Fuck your wife. That's why you gotta baby now.'

'You better get outta my face,' Ricky says dangerously.

Tre tries to intervene, but the brothers take no notice. Dough Boy pushes Ricky.

'You a punk,' he shouts. 'You been a punk since day one. Momma's boy.'

Ricky can't take this. He pushes Dough Boy back and charges at him. The two boys fall off the porch on to the grass wrestling and throwing punches. Tre rushes towards them and tries to break it up, but Chris shouts at him excitedly.

'Stay outta this Tre, this family business, this family business. Let em fight.'

Shanice comes out to the porch, holding little Ricky, and when she sees what's going on screams for Mrs Baker, who runs out of the house and straight towards the two young men. She springs at them, catching Dough Boy just as he's about to punch Ricky, and she hits him hard in the face. Dough Boy draws back, cursing. 'Shit.'

Ignoring him Mrs Baker fusses round Ricky who is getting up and shaking himself together.

'Ricky,' she says. 'Come here and let me see your face.'

But Ricky, angry and frustrated, fends her off.

'Naw, I'm going to the store.'

He hurries out to the sidewalk, Tre by his side. In his haste and anger he doesn't see the mailman who comes into the yard, walks up to Mrs Baker, and gives her three envelopes. One of them is a letter from the SAT Testing Bureau, and when Mrs Baker sees it she calls out after Ricky.

'Ricky. Ricky. The test scores. The test scores.'

But Ricky and Tre are already moving round the corner, and Mrs Baker turns back to the house. On the way she goes past Dough Boy who is standing holding the side of his face and staring at her.

'What you hit me for?' he says in a hurt, angry tone. 'What you hit me for?'

Mrs Baker keeps on going, not even acknowledging Dough Boy's question, her head and eyes pointing straight ahead as if he wasn't there.

Chris rolls across the yard in his chair towards

Dough Boy. He gives his friend a look of sympathy and concern.

'Hey, man. What she hit you for.'

Dough Boy shrugs him off and his face falls back into its usual hard and impassive lines.

'Shut up, nigga,' he says.

CHAPTER FIFTEEN

On the way to the store Ricky is still holding his face where Dough Boy hit him. He's still angry, his emotions churning inside him, and he tells Tre quickly that he's been thinking about getting away into the Army.

'Yo thinking about what?' Tre shouts. 'You gotta be a damn fool.'

Ricky explains earnestly.

'They say I can learn how to work computers and all that and they give me money for college.'

Tre shakes his head in disbelief.

'Look at ya, sound like the damn commercial. But they don't tell you that you don't belong to yourself no more. You join them you belong to the government. Like a slave, do what they say. Pops always told me Black man don't have no place in the Army.'

'See, I gotta think about my little boy and all,' Ricky keeps on. He's been thinking this out over the last few days. 'I don't wanna be like my brother and shit, hanging out not doing shit, end up dealing cane just like him. I want to do something, be somebody.'

Tre understands, but he needs to convince Ricky that he's mistaken.

'Man I'm telling you, you go in there you ain't gonna be nobody, not unless you get a college degree then at least you can be an officer.'

By this time they're at the store which is a typical Korean-ghetto corner store. On the side of the wall is a huge drawing of a Korean dragon and a painted sign which reads 'SEOUL TO SEOUL LIQUOR'. In front of the store there is the usual collection of drunks standing around talking, laughing, and sucking on bottles wrapped in brown paper. A couple of them rush the boys begging for change. On the way out the same thing happens, as if the drunks are so far gone that they can't remember what happened two minutes ago.

Ricky has bought three lottery tickets and he begins scratching them off. Ricky's never won anything, and he doesn't believe he will, but he keeps on hoping. The first one is a loser.

'You gotta be Mexican to win that shit,' Tre says.

'I win the lottery,' Ricky says, 'I won't have to worry about a goddamn thing. Don't haveta worry bout college, don't haveta worry bout no muthafucking seven hundred on the SAT. Don't haveta worry about shit.'

In every project in every poor neighbourhood all over the country people dream the same dream, and

126

Tre is about to say that when he catches sight of Ferris's red Hyundai prowling round the corner.

Ferris is driving, accompanied by a rap with a heavy bass line which vibrates through the car. He sees Tre and Ricky at the same time they see him. In the back seat his knucklehead buddies follow his gaze with rising excitement.

'There's that muthafucka,' they chorus.

'That was talking shit the other night,' one says.

'Yeah,' the other knucklehead says. 'I heard he was talking about your momma, your grandmomma, and called your sister a hoe bitch.'

Ferris doesn't believe any of this. It's just wind, but he knows it means they're urging him to go, and he puts his hand under his seat and pulls out a sawn-off shot-gun.

On the street, Tre and Ricky begin walking, moving faster and looking straight ahead. This is a drive-by situation, and they know also that Ferris is primed for Ricky. Tre's heart is thumping with fear and rage.

'When I say cut,' he tells Ricky, 'let's cut through these houses.'

He gives it a couple of beats. Then: 'Cut.'

The boys begin running, and they break through the nearest yard, separating to race along the two sides of the house. At the backyard fence Tre hears the pit-bulls growling and barking just as he is about to vault over into the next yard. He flashes Ricky a look and they climb up quickly, each of them on opposite sides of the backyard, and they walk the length of their separate fences, balancing like tight-rope walkers. Below them the pit-bulls on each side of the walls bark and leap up and down trying to reach the boys.

As Ricky and Tre disappear through the houses Ferris turns at speed into the next cross street, head-ing for the alley between the houses. In the middle of the street he goes past Mrs Baker's house where Dough Boy and his friends are sitting around drink-ing and talking. They watch the red Hyundai roll past and Monster makes a sound of disgust.

'That nigga roll up on the set one more time,' he says, 'I swear I'm gonna blast his ass.'

Dough Boy hears him but he isn't paying atten-tion. Something has struck him as soon as he saw the Hyundai speeding by. Dough Boy sits up and his eyes widen. He puts down the bottle of beer he was drinking, and walks out into the yard, gazing towards the corner round which the Hyundai had disappeared.

The homeboys look at him with curiosity. Dough Boy is acting strange, and for the moment, they can't work out why he's so interested in the Hyundai.

'What's wrong?' Chris calls out, but Dough Boy,

looking as if he can hear and see a vision that they can't, suddenly stiffens.

'Rick,' Dough Boy shouts.

He turns and runs for the house stumbling over Monster. 'Get the fuck out da way,' Dough Boy snarls.

In another moment he runs out again holding his pistol in his hand.

'Oh shit,' Chris says looking at him. 'Somebody going to get gatted.'

'I gotta find Rick,' Dough Boy shouts to the home-boys.

Monster and Dooky make a standing start.

'Yeah,' shouts Monster. 'Let's take these niggas out.'

They run after Dough Boy and jump into the Impala as he screeches off. Chris is left behind but he wheels himself on to the sidewalk and begins racing his chair as fast as it will go after Dough Boy's car.

Meanwhile Ricky and Tre have got through the backyards and jumped down from the walls into the alley. Both of the boys lean on the wall, which is covered with gang graffiti, trying to catch their breath. Ricky turns to urinate on the fence, just below the slogan which reads CRENSHAW MAFIA.

'I gotta drain the weasel,' Ricky says. 'Wanna see me write my name?'

Tre stares at him in disbelief.

'What? No. I don't wanna see you write your name. Hurry up, last thing I want to do is get shot waiting for your ass to piss.'

Ricky finishes. He's annoyingly casual, and Tre feels like a cat on hot bricks.

'Let's go this way,' he suggests.

'No, let's split up.'

'No, man,' Tre says, 'we shouldn't do that, if we gotta throw some heads it'd be better to be together.'

Ricky gives a careless laugh.

'Them fools ain't gonna squabble. They just trying to show out and shit. Besides we can run faster separately.'

Tre is in no mood to argue.

'I'll meet you at your house,' he says, and the two boys walk towards the opposite ends of the alley.

Ricky begins scratching off his lottery tickets as he goes. Carefree, even, now it's all over, a little exhilarated by the unexpected action. He's so busy with the lottery tickets that he doesn't see the Hyundai roll up across the mouth of the alley. The black-tinted window comes down slowly, and a shot-gun barrel pokes out. Behind it one of Ferris's knuckle-head buddies begins to take aim.

At the same moment Tre looks back and sees what is happening. He begins running back down the alley.

'Ricky. Ricky,' he shouts as he goes.

Ricky, alerted by Tre's shouts, looks up just in time to see the shot-gun aiming at him, and dropping his groceries he turns and begins to run. He's so fast that he makes more than a few yards before the knucklehead in the Hyundai reacts. Then the shot-gun blasts off like a cannon. Ricky is hit and he staggers but doesn't fall, continuing his last run up the alley. The shot-gun fires once more, and Ricky goes down slowly, his arms flailing in the air, the blood seeping from his riddled chest.

As Tre reaches Ricky and drops to his knees beside him, Dough Boy's Impala turns the corner, speeding, throwing up a cloud of dust. The window of the Hyundai rolls up, and Ferris zooms off.

Dough Boy stops the car a few yards away from where Tre is kneeling beside Ricky, and gets out calmly. Behind him the homeboys climb out. Monster leans on the car and bangs his fist on it. From the end of the alley Chris's wheelchair comes rolling. Dough Boy gets on his knees beside Tre and looks at his brother. Then he pulls Rick's body close to him. Both he and Tre are crying, the tears rolling down their faces, unnoticed. Around them people from the neighbourhood are coming to the walls of their backyards or out through the gates and into the alley to see what has happened. This is a familiar happening, but it still leaves them shocked and afraid. They mutter in low voices to each other.

Dough Boy doesn't know that they're there. He holds Ricky close one last time, then he raises himself from the ground still holding on to the body. He looks at Tre.

'Let's take him home,' he says.

CHAPTER SIXTEEN

Mrs Baker and Shanice are out of sight when Dough Boy pulls up in front of the house. Slowly and carefully he and Tre pull Ricky's body out of the passenger door, but then Dough Boy signals to Tre that he can carry his brother alone. Still cradling Ricky with the tenderest of care Dough Boy walks through the yard and up the steps, Tre by his side, and the rest of the homeboys following behind. In the street a crowd of people from the neighbourhood are beginning to gather, watching the little procession go into the house. Chris pushes through them along the sidewalk and rolls up to join his buddies on the porch.

Inside the house Dough Boy takes Ricky straight to the couch and lowers him carefully on to it. Hearing the commotion Shanice comes out of the kitchen with little Ricky in her arms, and immediately she sees the blood she begins screaming at the top of her voice. The baby begins crying too, setting up a loud wailing almost as loud as his mother's. She rushes for the couch and Tre tries to hold her back.

'Noooo. Noo God. Not Rick, please God.'

She struggles with Tre.

'Let me the fuck go.'

Just then Mrs Baker comes in.

'Girl,' she says lightly, 'what the hell's gotten into your ass?'

Immediately she takes it all in. Rick's body, the blood on Tre, and Dough Boy. She looks at Dough Boy, trying to be calm, although when she speaks it's on a rising note.

'What happened?' she says in a normal speaking voice. Then louder. 'What did you do to my son?'

Dough Boy holds her and she presses close to him shivering with shock and terror, then she pulls back and shouts into his face.

'What did you do to my son?'

'It wasn't my fault,' Dough Boy says in a pleading tone. But Mrs Baker slaps him violently, again and again, her face a mask of grief and hatred, then she whirls and throws herself to her knees beside the couch where Shanice and Tre are bent over Ricky. Tre gets out of the way and stands up with his head bowed. At the door Dooky and Monster are backing out towards the porch. Little Ricky is still crying with all the strength in his lungs and Dough Boy goes to take him from Shanice.

'Don't touch him,' she screams at him. 'Don't you ever touch him.'

'He don't need to be seeing this,' Dough Boy protests. But both Shanice and his mother hit out at him and he pulls away, his shoulders bent, dejection and grief written all over him. He moves back next to Tre and Tre takes his arm, facing up close to him. They look at each other with an intensity that charges the air around them.

'My house in five minutes,' Tre says.

He turns and walks away, moving fast. Dough Boy stands still staring, then cowers as Mrs Baker attacks him, throwing blows from every angle, as if she's trying to kill him. BAM. BAM. Dough Boy turns his head away and puts his hands up to block the blows, but his mother keeps on coming, striking out at him.

'What did you do to my son?' she screams. 'You killed him. You killed him.'

CHAPTER SEVENTEEN

By the time Tre leaves the house there's a large crowd outside. He walks through them as if they aren't there until Brandi comes out and walks along by his side tugging at his arm. But Tre doesn't slow down or even look at her. He has tears in his eyes and a cold blank stare on his face, and Brandi begins to feel a terrible fear that grabs her and turns her stomach over.

'Tre,' she says, beginning to shout, trying to get through to him. 'Tre. What happened. Did something happen to Rick? Did he get shot?'

Tre acts as if he hasn't heard, simply walking fast towards his house, and when Brandi pulls at his arm trying to stop him and make him pay attention, he pushes her away.

'Home. Go home,' he says in a thick, choking voice almost unrecognizable as his.

Furious pulls up and gets out of his car with a couple of bags of groceries in his hands as Tre goes into the house.

'Tre,' he calls out, 'help me with these bags. Tre. Tre.'

Tre keeps on walking into the house. Furious hefts the bags with a puzzled look, but before he can move Brandi moves over to him. Furious is her last, best hope to keep Tre from getting involved in these crazy shootings.

'Talk to him,' she pleads. 'Rick just got shot. Talk to Tre.'

Furious closes the door of the car and walks towards the house. This was one of his nightmares in the early days, he thinks, and just when it looked as if Tre was grown up, safe from the pitfalls of life in the neighbourhood, it had to happen. As he goes into the front door Tre is coming out the bedroom, the loaded .357 Magnum in his hand. Tre sees his father and stops. They face each other, both of them gathering their willpower for this struggle.

'What are you doing?' Furious asks. 'If you are gonna do this you are gonna have to shoot me first.'

Suddenly he's conscious that Brandi is still behind him, peeking through the half-open door. He turns and speaks to her kindly.

'He's all right. Go home. He'll call later.'

He closes the door and stands square in front of it again.

'Tre listen to me,' Furious says. 'I understand about your friend and all, and my heart goes out to his mother but that is their problem. You are my son, my problem. Now give me the muthafuckin gun.'

He holds his hand out and Tre hesitates, avoiding his father's eyes. Then, slowly, he hands him the gun. Furious takes, it unloads it and throws it on to the couch. He goes over to Tre and hugs him hard. In the circle of his father's arms Tre begins to cry like a child.

'You are my only son,' Furious says. 'I love you and I'm damned if I'm gonna lose you to this bullshit.'

There's a knock on the door. Furious guesses that it's Brandi, and he goes over to let her in, then walks out on to the porch.

Brandi rushes to Tre and embraces him. They're both crying, and he leads her into his bedroom where they sit on the bed. But Tre gets up and begins to pace the room. He wasn't able to resist his father. He never could, but this time he wanted to disobey him, even though he knew Furious was right. Right or wrong isn't it, he thinks. Ricky was my friend. I have to do something.

Meanwhile Furious faces Dough Boy who has pulled up and walked on to his porch.

'I heard about Rick. I'm sorry.'

'Yeah. Where's Tre?' Dough Boy asks bluntly.

Dough Boy's face is swollen with emotion, but his eyes are focused and set hard.

'He can't come out right now.' Unconsciously, Furious is using the same words he used when Dough Boy and Ricky came to the door when Tre was doing his chores or some piece of homework. He looks at Dough Boy closely. 'What you gonna do?'

'What do you think I'm gonna do?'

Doughboy looks him in the eye. Man to man.

'I guess you gonna do what you feel you have to do. You think it will make you feel better?'

Dough Boy thinks about the question.

'Yeah,' he says. 'Yeah. It will.'

He turns around to walk away, and Furious calls out after him.

'Darin.'

'What?'

'Just remember this,' Furious says. 'That's what they want you to do.'

Dough Boy respects Furious and he knows that he's talking sense. But this is not the right time, he thinks. Not when my brother's just been smoked. A man can't let them smoke his brother without doing something.

'Who's they?' he asks Furious. Then he turns and walks away on to the sidewalk towards his car.

Brandi is just coming out of the bathroom as Furious ends his conversation with Dough Boy. She goes back towards Tre's room and at the door she sees that he's gone. She goes further into the room to where she can see through the open window and she sees Tre jumping into Dough Boy's Impala.

Right away Brandi turns and runs into the livingroom where Furious is just coming in from the porch. He closes the front door and turns to face her, his face full of the concern he feels for Dough Boy and about what he's doing. Then his eyes meet Brandi's and he knows.

CHAPTER EIGHTEEN

It is a terrible night, a night where sorrow and rage hang over the neighbourhood like a dark cloud. On the Baker porch Shanice and Mrs Baker are standing watching as Ricky's body is rolled out to the coroner's wagon, its lights flashing. The women are silent. Shanice is sunk in dumb misery, and Mrs Baker is thinking that all her hopes of making her life mean something have vanished along with Ricky. She doesn't think about Dough Boy and where he might be. She doesn't blame him any more for Rick's death, but she has no hopes for him. Nothing will change and when he crosses her mind, all emotion deserts her, leaving only a numb feeling in its place. Later on she will open the envelope which contains Ricky's test score, and she will see that he's received 710, ten more than the 700 he needed.

Meanwhile Furious is sitting in his living-room twirling his metal relaxation balls. It's time for a workout, but somehow he doesn't have the heart to get down to the weights tonight. He wonders what he'll tell Tre's mother if anything happens.

'Damn,' he mutters quietly, wondering where Tre is. 'Damn.'

Tre is in Dough Boy's car rolling along Crenshaw. Dough Boy and Dooky search the night, their eyes moving continually back and forth, looking for the red Hyundai. Monster is preparing the hardware, loading up an AK47 assault-rifle. Tre looks at Monster and his hands moving confidently over the gun, then he looks at Dough Boy, who keeps his eyes focused straight ahead. Tre is lost in thought. He keeps remembering Furious driving through Compton with Ricky and him, and he remembers his words on that day. Tre keeps pictures of his anger and disappointment.

Suddenly he calls out to Dough Boy.

'Let me out.'

Everyone looks at Tre. His eyes meet Dough Boy's, and the car slides to a halt. Tre gets out without a word and runs for the nearby bus stop, while Dough Boy takes off again.

He doesn't find Ferris for a while, so Dooky suggests getting something to eat, then at last, in the parking lot of a hamburger joint, he sees the red Hyundai.

Ferris and his two knucklehead buddies are having a good time, talking and laughing. This is a celebration. Dough Boy's car creeps slowly up on them and they don't see him until the Impala is in point blank range. They turn to run, but it's too late. Monster leans out and sprays them with bullets from the AK47, and all of them go down wounded.

Dough Boy leaps out of the car carrying his .45 and walks straight over to them. The knuckleheads are crawling and groping with their arms as they try to get away. Doughboy shoots them carefully as he goes past. When he reaches Ferris Dough Boy kicks him viciously in the ass.

'Get up muthafucka,' Dough Boy says, kicking him again. He's half-way to tears. 'Turn your punk ass over.'

Ferris turns over. He is in the last extremes of pain and terror, pleading with Dough Boy and snarling defiance at one and the same time.

'Please. Please,' he sobs. 'Please. I didn't pull the trigger. Fuck you. Well, fuck you then.'

Dough Boy shoots him at point blank range. He unloads the entire clip, staring closely at Ferris as he does so. Then he stands there staring.

In the Impala, Monster and Dooky can hear police sirens and they are dancing with nerves and anxiety. 'Damn, I'm on parole, ain't this about a bitch,' Monster says.

'Come on, man. Come on. Let's get out of here,' Dooky and Monster shout, as Dough Boy stands immobile, staring at Ferris's corpse. At last he turns, runs for the car, and jumps in. He is moving at his usual speed, but there is a blank dead look in his eyes.

'Let's roll,' Monster says. Dough Boy turns the wheel, and they zoom on out of the parking lot.

CHAPTER NINETEEN

Tre pauses in front of Brandi's house. For the last twelve hours he's been living in a nightmare and now he's woken up and he wants to see Brandi, reassure her that he's all right. Same old Tre. But as he watches the lights go out. Her mother will have gone to bed, so he shakes his head and keeps on walking. He can telephone. Facing Furious will be a different matter and he slows down in front of the yard, almost reluctant to go in. Then he musters up his energy, crosses the yard, up the steps, and goes in.

He feels funny looking round the sitting-room. It's as if he's been away long enough for everything to change, become unfamiliar, and he stands there looking round the house as though he really has been gone for a very long time. As he stands Furious comes out into the hallway, sees Tre, gives an exhalation of relief, then remembers his anger and disapproval of the boy's actions. He turns, without a word and goes into his bedroom, slamming the door.

Tre looks at the closed door. He wants to explain,

apologize, turn off Furious's disappointment. Instead he goes into his room and lays on the bed.

CHAPTER TWENTY

The next morning Tre is out on his porch eating a pomegranate. He looks towards Mrs Baker's house, thinking about the events of the day. He can hardly believe that Ricky has gone and he's been playing a game in his mind, wishing yesterday away, as if it was a nightmare he'd just woken up from.

Across the street Dough Boy comes out and sits on the porch. He's holding a forty-ounce bottle of beer in his hand and sipping from it. When he sees Tre he gets up and walks over slowly. As he does so a skinny dopehead man comes up and asks him for some crack. Without pausing Dough Boy does the transaction, sliding the money into his pocket and moving on into Tre's yard. He joins him on the porch and sits without speaking. Tre looks at him and nods but he doesn't speak either. Somehow, it's as if there is too much to say.

Dough Boy is the one who eventually breaks the ice.

'Ya know he used to run that ball up the street all day. Twenty-four, seven, three hundred and sixty . . . We gonna have the funeral tomorrow. My momma want you to say some words, since y'all was so tight.'

His voice trails off then he looks round and starts again.

'Y'know this is the first I been up this early in a long time. Turned on the TV this morning, news was on, they had this thing on living in a violent world y'know? Showed all these pictures of these foreign places y'know where foreigners live and all?'

Tre stirs for the first time. He looks round at Dough Boy.

'You mean like Lebanon and Israel, the Middle East?'

'Yeah, shit like that,' Dough Boy says. 'And I started thinking y'know. they either don't know, don't show, or don't care what goes on in the hood. They had all that foreign shit instead. They didn't show nothing about my brother.'

Tre thinks that this might be one of his father's thoughts, but he doesn't say so. Dough Boy begins to cry. All of his pent up rage and grief flowing through his eyes. Tre puts his hand on Dough's shoulder and gives him the napkin he's been using, the juice of the pomegranate staining it red. Dough Boy wipes his eyes slowly.

'I don't even have a brother no more,' he says.

'Don't have no momma either. She loved that fool more'n me anyways. Shit.'

Irrationally Tre thinks about the three people about whose love he is certain, and it crosses his mind how terrible it would be if they hadn't been part of his life.

Just then from the sidewalk Sheryl the crack addict calls out to Dough Boy. She's been watching him from the street, and now she ventures into the yard, desperate.

'Got some blow?'

'No bitch,' Dough Boy says repelling her with a gesture. 'And keep that baby out the motherfucking street. Shit.'

'I was crying all last night,' Tre says. 'Cried so much, it's almost like I ain't no more tears left. Ya know?'

Dough Boy gives him a serious look. His voice is sympathetic.

'Ya know, cuzz,' he says, 'I understand why you got out da ride last night. You didn't even need to be there in the first place. You gonna be moving up and all. Don't want that shit to come back and haunt your ass.'

Tre nods. He turns and looks at Dough Boy.

'Y'all got em?'

Dough Boy doesn't answer, simply looks at Tre, as if this was a question that didn't need to be asked.

Tre nods soberly.

'I don't even know how to feel about that now neither,' Dough Boy says. 'It just goes on. Next thing you know somebody might try to smoke me. It don't matter though, cause we all gotta go some time. Seem like somebody punched the wrong clock on Rick though.'

He shakes his head.

'I gotta go, cuzz.'

He gets up, grips Tre's hand and turns to walk away. Tre gets up and catches up with him before he goes.

'You still got one brother left,' he says.

Dough Boy smiles.

'I'll remember dat,' he says.

EPILOGUE

Dough Boy lived to see his brother buried the next day. Two weeks later he was murdered. Tre went to Moorehouse College where he majored in communications, with Brandi across the way at Spellman.

BOYZ N THE HOOD

INCREASE THE PEACE

All Pan books are available at your local bookshop or newsagent, or can be ordered direct from the publisher. Indicate the number of copies required and fill in the form below.

Send to: **CS Department, Pan Books Ltd., P.O. Box 40, Basingstoke, Hants. RG21 2YT.**

or phone: 0256 469551 (Ansaphone), quoting title, author and Credit Card number.

Please enclose a remittance* to the value of the cover price plus: 60p for the first book plus 30p per copy for each additional book ordered to a maximum charge of £2.40 to cover postage and packing.

*Payment may be made in sterling by UK personal cheque, postal order, sterling draft or international money order, made payable to Pan Books Ltd.

Alternatively by Barclaycard/Access:

Card No. | | | | | | | | | | | | | | | |

Signature:

Applicable only in the UK and Republic of Ireland.

While every effort is made to keep prices low, it is sometimes necessary to increase prices at short notice. Pan Books reserve the right to show on covers and charge new retail prices which may differ from those advertised in the text or elsewhere.

NAME AND ADDRESS IN BLOCK LETTERS PLEASE:

....

Name————————————————————————

Address————————————————————————

————————————————————————

————————————————————————

————————————————————————